MW01319146

Esterlynn

Psalm 34:8
Taste and see that the Lord is good.

Amy Heidenreich

WESTBOW PRESS
A DIVISION OF THOMAS NELSON & ZONDERVAN

WestBow Press books may be ordered through booksellers or by contacting:

WestBow Press
A Division of Thomas Nelson & Zondervan
1663 Liberty Drive
Bloomington, IN 47403
www.westbowpress.com
1 (866) 928-1240

ISBN: 978-1-4908-4707-8 (sc)
ISBN: 978-1-4908-4708-5 (hc)
ISBN: 978-1-4908-4706-1 (e)

Library of Congress Control Number: 2014913996

Printed in the United States of America.

WestBow Press rev. date: 08/25/2014

It is my great honor to dedicate this book to my earliest fan and constant encourager, Sandy.

Thanks, Mom, I love you!

Prologue

Ellen Sattler was experiencing that familiar oxymoronic sensation that came over her every time at this point in the process: the sadness of wanting to hang on welded with the eagerness of knowing it was time to let go.

She mingled comfortably with the eleven families that were nearing the final stage of adoption in China. It was standard practice for a group such as this to meet in Beijing for orientation and initial paperwork before traveling to the province where their children would be readied to meet them. The final portion of the process took place at the US Consulate here in Guangdong Province, where parents would receive their child's Chinese visa, allowing them entry to the United States.

Ellen was a Chinese American living her dream job of working with adoptive families. She'd been working with the international adoption agency for nearly three years now and continued to be blessed by every couple, seeing the joy that they experienced when holding their child for the first time. She felt privileged to witness the bonding process that took place over the two-week span of time that she spent with them as she helped to process paperwork, assisted with health issues, and escorted the families to the medical center for the requisite checkup prior to leaving China.

The White Swan Hotel in Guangzhou was advertised as one of the leading hotels in the world, located on Shamian Island with its gorgeous setting along the Pearl River. This luxurious hotel was where the families from Ellen's agency always stayed during this final stage of red tape. Families had time to shop at local stores that were walking distance from the hotel; nearby jade markets and other tourist attractions added to their experience of the Chinese culture. Quite often, the restaurants in the area proved the most appreciated attractions; many hosted the closest thing to Western food that the families had experienced since leaving the States.

Couples of a wide mix were always represented, with their ages ranging from early thirties to sixties. Some were second-, third-, even fourth-time returnees with older adopted children along for the union with their new sibling. The current adoptees typically ranged in age from nine months to two years, although some families adopted older children who were generally special-needs cases.

This particular group was pulsing with the added layer of excitement of knowing they would be home, new addition in tow, just before Christmas. They were gathered in the bar area of the lounge, chatting cheerily while draining glasses of cool refreshment before their walk to the consulate. Petite, young waitresses in Santa-style dresses and matching hats glided gracefully among the consumers.

Ellen chatted easily with the families; her favorite part was holding the babies. She loved to give the new parents a break every now and then, since the bonding experience could be exhausting at times, especially if a child tended to cling to one parent over the other. Such was the case with Karl and Janice; Karl was a giant man with a heart to match. Many of these children had only known the care of women and would take time to warm up to *Big Daddy*. Yet they always did.

Ellen was bouncing their ten-month-old girl as another adoption agency rep arrived to walk the parents to the consulate.

She stroked the baby's cheek with the back of her hand and whispered, "Soon, little Sarah, you'll be on your way to your new home in the United States." She reluctantly handed the precious bundle back to Janice just as her cell phone rang. Ellen checked her caller ID before excusing herself. As she answered her phone, a sweet smile pulled at her lips. "Wei, Cheng."

Ellen waved a farewell as she walked away from the group but was still within earshot to hear Janice say to her husband, "I think that Cheng has called her before." She looked Sarah in the eye and kissed her on the tip of her nose before adding, "Mommy suspects Miss Ellen needs a good man."

Ellen walked as she talked. Parts of the conversation were in Mandarin, but Cheng knew she was still a novice with the language and cordially switched to English. They firmed up plans to meet in a couple of hours in the White Swan's lobby. The conversation ended with their unusual yet intimate exchange. She pressed the phone closer to her ear, leaning into his words. "God is good, Ellen."

She responded with a joyful laugh that settled into a soft sigh. "All the time, Cheng. All the time." Ending the call, Ellen noticed that she was standing by the gigantic Christmas tree in the foyer of the hotel. It stood at least thirty feet tall alongside the cascading waterfall with the pagoda at the top. A combination of mist from the falls and tears from the past formed in her eyes. Christmas always made her think of Esterlynn and the amazing transformation that God had done in her heart all those years ago.

Waves of nostalgia washed over her as she rode the elevator to her room on the fifteenth floor. Letting herself in with her key card, she walked over to the window and looked down on the Pearl River. She touched the pin on the lapel of her jacket with the same appreciation she always felt, a reminder of God's goodness. Having two hours before her meeting with Cheng, Ellen decided to make herself some tea and do something she rarely permitted. She firmly believed that reliving the past often served as a roadblock to the present, but every now and then, it was good to look back on the faithfulness of God. With a cup of hot tea warming her hands, she settled in and allowed her mind drift back to the events that led up to that Christmas back when she was ten. It all started in the spring of that same year, in a cemetery of all places.

One

Her body shivered again, this time strong enough to break through her unconscious state. At first, Ellen had allowed herself to imagine it was all part of a dream, but this latest shudder roused her enough to notice the cold dampness that had crept into the ground beneath her. She'd fallen asleep on her side with her knees pulled up to her chest, arms stacked under her head as a pillow.

She opened her eyes slightly and forced back a cry as she saw long arms stretched wide in silhouette against the dark sky. She felt so small and defenseless with her back pressed against a cold, hard surface. As memory swallowed confusion, relief rushed in right behind it. She was still in the cemetery. The shadowy image was the depiction of a crucifix and her back was cramped from the gravestone that had doubled as a bed.

There were shadows everywhere, each with its own hidden haunt. This cemetery, the after-dark version, bore little resemblance to the one she and her sister Brynn used to explore in the daytime when they were younger.

They'd spent endless hours walking through its fascinating history, calculating the life span of each marker and providing vivid commentary. Ellen recalled the first time they'd seen the marker whose birth year equaled its end. "This poor thing died before her first birthday. Oh, the heartache!" Ellen would make such pronouncements with an air of solemnity beyond her years.

Yes, being brave in the cemetery had proven easy with her big sister in broad daylight. But Brynn wasn't here now. She was probably busy with homework, totally unaware that her little sister had made a harebrained decision to come home from her friend Emily's house without telling either of their parents.

The friends had planned a sleepover but Ellen had been overwhelmed with a feeling of homesickness. She'd slipped out for home, taking a shortcut through the cemetery rather than staying on the familiar roads. The sun had already been setting its sights on dismissing the day yet Ellen had convinced herself it was a good idea. After all, she knew her way around, right?

The last thing she remembered tonight was passing that same marker with the familiar yet mystifying words etched across its smooth surface.

Our Few Days with You
Will Sustain Us for Now;
Till We Meet in Heaven,
As God Allows.

A mixture of jealousy and confusion had risen within Ellen the first time the sisters had read it. The parents of this infant had actually *wanted* their child only to have her suddenly taken away. How could they hold onto hope of heaven with the God who had caused such grief?

Ellen knew she was blessed to have been adopted by Brynn's parents, but some days her heart and her head didn't agree. Abandonment by her birth parents was a hard fact to overlook. Bitterness crept in like a masked bandit on those days. And when it did, Ellen found the message on that tombstone confusing at best, a scam at worst.

She sat up now, looking every which way. She must have really wandered because in all her exploring with her sister, she'd never seen the eerie, hulking cross with the body of Jesus fixed in stone, eyes forever gazing down in perfect agony for all who passed below. She shivered and wrapped herself in a hug, pushing her hands into opposite sleeves in an effort to keep them warm.

Even as she told herself she wouldn't cry, she could feel the tears building up and threatening to spill over. She used that well of wetness as excuse for what she saw now. Something was hovering about thirty feet out, between a budding tree and a grave with plastic flowers on each side. There was no way of knowing the color of the flowers, as dark and cloudy as it was, yet the ones near the tree grew bright enough to reveal shades of yellow and blue, because of the *light*. Ellen had to assume it was the repressed waterworks playing games with her vision. She blinked quickly, allowing the restrained tears to escape down her cheeks. Her vision cleared and what she saw should have frightened her, yet it didn't.

The light moved slowly closer to Ellen. It emitted no heat yet its brightness actually made her feel warm. She pulled herself to her feet with thoughts of running or at least screaming. Yet she stood still. The impulse to cry was forgotten even as the tears remained wet on her face. The need to breathe was dismissed for the moment.

All at once, a voice spoke from the light. "Don't be afraid."

The reality of the situation came to a climax. She was cold and lost, her sister unreachable, surrounded by death after dark—alone. All these things welled up inside as she took two steps back and cried out, "What do you want?"

"I am here to bring you out of the darkness," the voice replied. "I am here to bring you home."

The tears returned quickly and her lips trembled as Ellen whispered sharply, "I *do* want to go home! But the darkness is frightening me and I can't find my way!"

"Learn to walk in the light," the voice said. "Darkness covers but light always reveals truth."

Ellen felt confused and hopeful all at once. She thought of Brynn and home, but with a sense of peace now, as she somehow knew she was safe. As she regained her two steps, the light started to lead the way. It advanced little by little, but never more than a few steps at a time, always near enough to light her path.

No longer afraid, Ellen asked bravely, "What's your name?"

At first she thought she would get no response, so long was the wait for an answer. But the light slowed and hovered for a moment as a voice said, "I have no name, but if it gives you comfort to attach my existence in such a way, you may choose one for me."

The light began to move again, guiding her way, and as she followed, she frowned for a moment, thinking about that grave that spoke of heaven. She closed her eyes tightly, picturing the name elegantly scrawled into the stone's surface, and smiled in remembrance. It was somehow perfectly fitting to attach it to her guide, a new friend that would always speak of truth and light.

Her face brightened as she claimed it aloud. "Then I will call you Esterlynn!"

Two

Morning sunlight warmly caressed Ellen's face. Her bedroom blinds were open. It was her mother's doing, a gentle nudge into a new day. She reveled in the comfort of her bed and its covering, imagining the handmade quilt arrayed in Chinese calligraphy, even before opening her eyes to its bright colors and perfect stitching. She rolled to her back and yawned, tugging at the remnants of her dream. Except it wasn't a dream. She opened her lips only enough for one whispered word to escape. "Esterlynn!"

On her feet in a flash, Ellen ran down the stairs two at a time in her excitement to tell about her new friend. She heard the distant tones of the radio in the kitchen, undoubtedly playing her mom's favorite Christian station. Terri Sattler turned from her pancake prep in time for her daughter's entrance, which was anything but graceful in its urgency. Any hope for a warm greeting was demolished when Ellen saw her mom's face, anger etched into those lines prone to display her dissatisfaction.

Ellen almost visibly shrunk as she realized she'd never checked in with her mom upon letting herself in last night via the garage door's keyless entry. She decided to busy herself pulling plates out of the cupboard, knowing her mom wouldn't hear anything Ellen had to say until she'd unleashed the verbal tirade that went with that look. Trying desperately to side-step her indiscretion, she took a deep breath and plunged in, her words leading her thoughts, which happened often. "I met a new friend, Mom. Her name is Esterlynn!"

Her mom poured pancake batter onto the sizzling hot griddle as she responded. "We'll talk about *new* friends after I'm convinced that I can trust the ones you have already!" She lifted the edges of the pancakes as she continued. "Lucky for both you and Emily, her mother called this morning and filled me in on your little covert plan. Imagine how surprised I'd have been otherwise—going into your room that's supposed to be empty and finding you sleeping peacefully in your bed!"

"I'm so sorry, Mom! I should have called you. I guess I forgot. But listen, Mom. The whole reason I made it home at all last night was because of Esterlynn! She helped me when I got lost in the cemetery after leaving Emily's."

Suddenly, Ellen had her mom's full attention. "How many times have I told you not to cut through the cemetery after dark?" The conversation gate was closing fast as her mom let out an angry sigh and said, "We'll discuss this later. Now go find Brynn. These cakes are almost ready."

Ellen turned angrily on her heel and went down the hall to the den where she'd surely find Brynn on her laptop working on some paper for school. She tried to stomp her bare feet on the plush carpet as she walked in. True to form, Brynn was sitting primly on the edge of the desk chair, clicking away at the keys. In her own world, Brynn didn't hear her sister's first announcement for breakfast, so Ellen took it upon herself to make sure she heard the next one. Standing less than two feet behind her sister's chair, she yelled, "Time for breakfast!"

Lunging forward in surprise, Brynn's only save from falling was the very fact that the chair's wheels were set into the carpet. "Geez, Ellen! What's gotten into you?"

Still pouting, Ellen said, "I only met the most exotic and amazing friend last night and all Mom can think about is how I broke the rules!"

Brynn saved her file and stood as she said, "Ellen, Mom told me you snuck out last night without telling an adult. She doesn't need this from you, especially when Dad's on one of his trips."

"But Brynn, you're missing the point! Esterlynn—" But Ellen's words were cut short as they both heard their mom from the kitchen. "Girls! Now!"

Breakfast had been fairly silent; cleanup was hurried. Now from the backseat of the family's Ford Explorer, Ellen pressed her forehead against the window, hoping upon hope that she would catch a glimpse of Esterlynn as they drove past the cemetery on the way to church. Nothing. What did she even remember after she'd started following her new and trusted friend last night? Not much. Just that sense of feeling safe and then waking up in her bed this morning.

Her mom signaled and turned the car into the parking lot of their home church. It was busy and filled with airy greetings tossed at other members as they filed down the aisle to their usual pew. Her mom extended quick hugs and handshakes even as Ellen noted the fairly well-hidden tightness in her mother's frame. She received one quick glance as they sat down. It was the familiar we'll-talk-about-this-later look that Ellen had come to know well.

After the welcome and announcements, the congregation sang dutifully from the standard hymnal. Brynn was a sophomore in high school and would stay through the entire adult service, but Ellen, being only in fifth grade, would head to the children's Sunday school area after the children's sermon. Ellen was in the middle of reminiscing about her chance encounter with Esterlynn when Pastor Steve called the kids to come forward. She saw a couple of kids from her class and sat crisscross-applesauce next to Kendra on the carpet, her eyes drifting to the cross centered above the altar.

"Good morning, kids," said Pastor Steve.

About a dozen kids ranging from three to eleven peeled out age-appropriate responses. Being in tune to kids, and realizing the older kids were feeling a bit "advanced" for the children's sermon, the pastor had recently maneuvered a way to draw them in by asking for a volunteer to reread portions of the daily gospel.

Ellen's attention had been caught swiftly during the initial reading, so when Pastor Steve asked for a volunteer, she was at the ready. Her hand rose rapidly in the fashion of a respectful salute.

"Well, Ellen, so glad to see you excited about God's Word this morning. Our reading is from Matthew, chapter 18, verses 10 through 12."

Few kids actually brought their Bibles and Ellen was no exception. Reaching out to borrow the pastor's, she began to read.

See that you do not look down on one of these little ones. For I tell you that their angels in heaven always see the face of my Father in heaven. What do you think? If a man owns a hundred sheep and one of them wanders away, will he not leave the other ninety-nine on the hills and go to look for the one that wandered off?

Most of the kids seemed bored or distracted as she quickly returned the Bible, but Ellen was leaning forward, nearly biting her tongue off as she held back her questions.

Pastor Steve seemed determined to torture her as he paused calmly, allowing his gaze to rest briefly on each face. At long, laboring last, he began to speak. "Have any of you ever been lost or maybe felt lost?" he asked.

Again, her hand shot up, quicker than any other, but Pastor Steve opted to give someone else a turn. "Riley, tell me about the time you were lost."

Five-year-old Riley went into mind-numbing detail about the time he and his mom had been separated for an eternity (in little Riley's interpretation) at the local supermarket. Several other kids were called on to share similar stories while Ellen tried to suppress her frustration, feeling forced to stifle what she considered the ultimate story of lost and found.

Pastor Steve talked about Jesus being our Good Shepherd and how he does not want even one person to remain lost and separate from him and his Father in heaven. Next he asked for examples of how we as Christians can reach out to the lost and where we even look for them. Ellen sensed her time was running out and raised her hand without any intention of answering his question, only planning to volley back with her own.

The backlog of waiting that morning, beginning with her severed conversation with her mom, pushed her to blurt out a question of shirttail relevance.

"What about angels? I read about angels in there somewhere. Do angels help people that are lost too?" Her deep-brown eyes had an almost frantic intensity as she waited for his response, her chest rising and falling quickly in short breaths.

Some of the older kids looked at her as if she were a nut case. Pastor Steve patiently dealt with her outburst, explaining that the verse does in fact say that children have angels in heaven that are watching over them. However, the message of today's gospel reading was about *Jesus* searching out the lost, *not* angels.

A tiny, stubborn frown crept between Ellen's eyebrows as she fired her next question. "But the Bible must have other stories about angels guiding people?" She leaned back, arms crossed firmly across her chest, daring him to deny it.

"Well," he said, "there are many stories of angels in the Bible, and one in particular comes to mind in Exodus 23, where the Lord tells Moses that he is going to send an angel ahead of Moses and the Israelites to lead them into the land that God has prepared. However, in order to stay on topic today—"

The rest of his words reached Ellen's ears in a "waaah-wa-waaah-wa-waaah" fashion similar to Charlie Brown's reception of his teacher in the famous cartoon. One screaming thought pulsed in her mind: *Esterlynn is an angel! She led me out of that cemetery last night, just like the angel that led Moses. I am sure of it!*

After the service, Ellen's mom was sipping a cup of black coffee with groups of other congregants when someone to her left touched her elbow and said, "Terri Sattler, how are you, girlfriend?"

Terri turned, looking into the face of Barb Malone. The women had known each other since they were Ellen's age, having met at this very church in Sunday school class. Barb was a successful real estate agent in the area, wife of the local sheriff and with no kids after fifteen years of marriage. She was a tall, fashion-plate blonde with impeccable taste in clothes, perfect nails, and a smile of genuine love that crushed anyone's attempt to call her conceited in her beauty.

"Life is good," said Terri, carefully balancing her hot coffee while giving her old friend a quick hug. After all these years, Terri felt that familiar rise of self-consciousness as she stood next to her drop-dead-gorgeous sister in Christ. Terri herself—mother of two, part-time yoga instructor, and wife of a husband on the road most weeks—felt anything but glamorous in her sensible clothes, low-maintenance nails, and self-colored hair (*autumn gold*, according to the box).

"Is Jack in LA again?" asked Barb with her usual frown of concern mixed with empathy.

"He should be home on Friday, but as always, that's subject to change," said Terri with an attempt to sound matter-of-fact. Her husband had worked as a corporate engineer for a papermaking company for almost ten years now. Jack had made a few trips to the Los Angeles area over the years, but United Paper now required him to work nearly full-time at the regional site in LA, increasing his travel extensively in the past year. California was a far cry from their small rural community in Wisconsin, as the family was well learning.

"I'll be honest, Terri," said Barb. "As much as I worry about Tom and the dangers of his job, I am very grateful to have him home in bed with me every night. It must be so hard taking care of those two girls virtually on your own. You know it goes without saying that if there's anything at all that you need, I'm here for you, my friend."

"Thanks, Barb. It's so nice to know I can count on you." But even as Terri said this, they both knew it would take the most extreme of straits for her to ask for help. Terri was an independent woman, which proved to be a tricky fulcrum on the teeter-totter of strength and weakness.

Three

Later that night, with Ellen tucked away sleeping and Brynn undoubtedly checking out the latest all-important updates on Facebook, Terri reflected on her exchange with Ellen after church. She sat on the window seat of hers and Jack's bedroom, massaging lotion into her feet, wishing once again that he was here while in the same instant feeling weak for needing him.

Terri had finally taken the time to listen to Ellen's whole story after she had established Ellen's punishment for breaking the rules: two full weeks of dishwasher duty, which worked out wonderfully for Brynn, along with a hefty one-week grounding. As it turned out, Terri's concern for Ellen's safety and carelessness was soon outweighed by her worry over Ellen's need to create an imaginary friend (or *angel,* as Ellen insisted).

"Lord," said Terri aloud, "what am I going to do with that girl? I know it was your divine will for her to be matched with our family. So why do I feel like I can't get anything right with her? What am I supposed to be doing for her?" But even as she prayed, she knew the answer. That same soft voice spoke to her heart with the one answer to all her questions: *love her unconditionally.*

But how could she support this latest fantasy? Terri was far too sensible to believe that Ellen had actually had an encounter with an angel, a divine messenger from God! And oh how easy it would be to blame her daughter's heightened imagination on

Jack! He was always encouraging the girls to be dreamers while Terri was the family pillar of common sense.

Seemingly on cue, the phone on her nightstand lit up, voicing its chirpy ring in a passive-aggressive request to be answered. She pushed the talk button. "Hey Jack," she said, trying not to sound as tired and discouraged as she felt.

"Hi, sweet," was his response from some three thousand miles away. She bristled slightly at his term of endearment. How convenient for him to be simply missing her while she was dealing with the stickiness of their lives back here at home! But just as quickly, she felt that check in her spirit that was becoming more and more regular as she was learning (only by the grace of God) to be less self-focused.

"How was your day, honey?" she asked, trying her best to shove all her own worries to the back burner for a moment.

"Oh, the usual: endless meetings and conference calls, but overall, a successful day." And in his endearing (and almost saint-like) fashion, he switched gears to ask how things were for her and the girls.

"Brynn had a great time at the spring dance on Friday night; that Josh seems like a very nice boy. I took lots of pictures. And of course we had church today. I talked with Barb for a while; Tom is training a new deputy. Sounds like he has potential."

A short pause hung over the line, and then Jack said, "I'm so disappointed that I couldn't be there for Brynn's big night. I bet she looked beautiful." There was a longer pause before he continued. "And what about Ellen? How is she?"

"Ellen is Ellen. We had a bit of an issue today. Nothing you need to be concerned about," said Terri in her usual everything's-taken-care-of-you-don't-have-to-worry-about-anything tone.

"Talk to me, Terri. What happened?" Jack asked with evident concern.

"Well, she decided to leave Emily's last night without telling me and took a moonlit stroll through the cemetery on her way home. We had a long talk and I feel pretty confident it won't happen again," Terri said with firmness. She hoped by keeping the focus on the misdemeanor, Jack would assume that was Terri's only concern. She let out a mental sigh of relief as he bit on it; no need to tell him about the angel incident. Personally, she was hoping the whole thing would be forgotten by the time he came home.

The conversation drew to a close as Jack promised to follow up with Ellen the next time they talked. The usual miss-you and love-you were shared with the heavy hearts of friends and lovers weighted by the acceptance that their marriage had become long distance, more often than not.

Upon returning the phone to its base, Terri threw up one last prayer as she crawled under the comforter on her side of the bed. "Lord, watch over our family and unite us in your grace."

Four

The next morning, Ellen was sitting on the comfortable wooden bench her dad had made, positioned at the end of their long driveway among the oak and maple trees with their leaves full out. The temperature was cool at 7:45 a.m. but promising to heat up by afternoon. Spring is often bypassed in Wisconsin, and late May often brags of temperatures approaching the eighties.

Less than a minute passed before Ellen was on her feet, pacing back and forth across the end of the driveway, impatiently watching for the first sign of the bus popping up over the hill. After making what she considered zero progress with her mom the night before, Ellen was eager to confer with her friend Emily on the whole situation; surely Emily would be excited for her! More importantly, Emily would believe her, because best friends don't just believe, they believe *in you!* Everyone else might think your dreams were far-fetched and ridiculous, but not your BFF. The whole world may think your goals are impossible, but not your BFF. Every kid in school might think you're different or full of strange ideas, but not your BFF.

But even with these thoughts in mind, her excitement waned and she slumped back onto the bench. This one really was out there, even for Emily. Ideas of angel rescue in the cemetery. Seriously! Could she really expect her BFF to believe this one? She'd missed the initial sight of the bus as it cleared the summit of the hill, caught up as she'd been in this passing cloud of discouragement.

As she reached the top step of the bus, the driver sped up, his schedule apparently a higher priority than the safety of the children. Using her sea legs, Ellen progressed down the aisle. She spied the smiling face of her faithful friend, framed in wiry corkscrew curls; any momentary doubt whisked away.

Emily looked at Ellen intently from behind her trendy purple-framed glasses. Leaning in with typical BFF all-knowing perception, she asked with a conspiratorial whisper, "I know you got busted for not calling; so did I. But does your mom know the rest of the story? Did you cut through the cemetery like you planned?"

That was one of many things Ellen loved about Emily; she always got right to the point. "Yeah, and I'm grounded for a week because of it. But listen. The bigger picture of my trip through the dead lands is what we really need to talk about!"

And Emily responded with another quick cut to the chase. "We have less than ten minutes to school, so you'd better spill it quickly!" Ellen felt that usual surge of love toward her friend and paused long enough to allow this much-needed affirmation to refill her heart before rushing into her story, no detail untold.

An impossibly long span of time dragged on after Ellen finished speaking and waited. She knew better than to rush Emily when she had that look on her face, the one that said she was in her "processing box." But her patience was rewarded, even as the bus pulled into the school's driveway. "There is obviously only one thing to do," Emily said matter-of-factly as she slouched into her backpack. "We'll sneak out tonight after everyone's in bed and meet at the cemetery. I simply *must* meet Esterlynn! One kid's eyewitness account may be easy to blow off, but two? Not a chance!"

Later that night (by Ellen's watch, it was well after midnight), the BFFs huddled together under Emily's worn and faded *Dora the Explorer* blanket. She was so grateful for her friend's common sense in bringing the ratty old thing because the temperature had dropped considerably after dark and the ground was already starting to take on a dewy dampness.

They'd arrived earlier with an air of rebellion and an optimistic sense of expectation. Flashlight beams danced back and forth among the tombstones as they'd wandered through rows upon rows of graves. Eventually, prudence dictated they conserve their batteries as the girls settled down under Jesus' outstretched arms, where Ellen had first seen Esterlynn.

After a few attempts at miscellaneous chitchat, the friends had lapsed into a noiseless vigil of waiting. A sufficient amount of pondering in darkness passed before Emily broke the silence, trying with all her might not to sound doubtful. "Are you sure this is the exact spot where you first saw her?"

"I should have known you wouldn't believe me either!" Ellen cried in a muffled but cross complaint. Even in the darkness, with no way of seeing the look on her friend's face, Ellen could sense the hurt she had inflicted with her careless words and hurriedly went on to add, "Oh Emily, I'm sorry! I know with all my heart that you believe me! I'm just so disappointed that Esterlynn has not come back!"

And maybe it was just that—disappointment, or perhaps a bit of guilty conscience for sneaking out to the very place which had initiated her recent grounding. Just as likely, it was a simple case of being tired and cold. Whatever the reason, Ellen found herself bursting into tears right there under the Dora blanket, sensing that same creepy gaze from the crucifix looking down on her. She turned her face upward in the general direction of her Savior and poured out the silent question in her heart. *Okay, Jesus, who's to believe me now?*

Five

Gwen was sitting on her back porch swing, toes scuffing absently against the concrete slab beneath her hot pink Crocs as she slowly rocked herself. Her short hair with its loose, gray curls blew slightly with the breeze as a slight frown caused a cloud to cross over her face, dimming her typically bright countenance. The conversation she'd had with Terri earlier that day was still bothering her. More drama with Ellen, this was not new or surprising.

Gwen pulled in a deep breath and let it out slowly, her eyes taking a moment to revel in the beauty of her backyard. Daffodils bobbed their yellow heads, leading the procession for other flowering plants to join in the season's bloom. The bright-green symphony of spring was everywhere, accompanied by the collective hum of distant lawnmowers.

The furrow that had crept between her brows flattened a bit as she allowed herself to reflect on one of her first meetings with Ellen at the diner. She and Ellen had been meeting there weekly for Tuesday night dinner since Ellen was five years old. That was when Terri had started teaching her one evening class at the yoga center (until then all her classes had been during the day while the girls were at school). Brynn, approaching twelve at the time, was just old enough to stay home alone while Gwen and Ellen had their bonding time.

Little Ellen had walked into the diner, taking in every detail of the rustic, north woods theme, from the log-style counter and chairs to the bears and pine trees stenciled along the wall near the ceiling. The thing that always intrigued Ellen most was the magnificent twelve-point buck mounted above the fireplace.

"Auntie Gwen, why do they have that dead deer up there?" She asked this with a look of wonder and disgust mixed together. Gwen had tried to explain that there was an overpopulation of deer in Wisconsin. Because of this, hunters were allowed to go out every fall to help reduce death from starvation that was inevitable, if the herds weren't thinned out.

"But why do they have to hang the head up there, staring at us? It's creepy!"

Rather than try to justify the whole sport side of the hunting habit in the area, Gwen chose to simply agree with Ellen as she steered her toward a table that put them a good distance from the whole grisly subject.

"So your daddy may start flying to Los Angeles soon for work," Gwen stated in an attempt to change the subject.

"I guess so. I guess that's in California. That's southwest of here, you know," Ellen announced with the authority of a teacher. "I wonder which way they fly to get there?" she mused aloud.

"Well, sweetie, you just said LA is southwest of here so—" But Gwen's geography lesson was truncated as Ellen interrupted.

"Oh, that doesn't mean anything, Auntie Gwen. Mommy says to get to China you fly north. I keep asking if you can see Santa's workshop from up there but no one gives me a real answer!" Ellen's voice grew louder and higher with frustration at this obvious obstruction of justice.

Gwen laughed aloud at the seriousness of her young niece and said, "Well, I suppose the closest I've ever been to the North Pole is when I visit my friend Muriel; she owns a B & B in the Upper Peninsula of Michigan. It's in a small town called St. Ignace, just across the lake from Mackinac Island. Maybe someday I could take you there."

A sharp, quick beep forced Gwen's thoughts back to her own backyard as her wristwatch announced the 5:00 p.m. hour. Easing herself from the porch swing, she winced a bit at the arthritic pain that had started settling into her knees in the past couple years. Even now, Gwen chuckled as she recalled that conversation. She had tried to explain to Ellen that China wasn't north of Wisconsin, only to be shot down again and again by Ellen's insistence that her parents had flown north on retrieving her from her birth country. But it was Gwen who learned a lesson later when Jack clarified that flying over the top of the globe was indeed the shortest route to China from Wisconsin. That Ellen was a sharp cookie even at five years old. So who was to say for sure that she had not actually encountered an angel in the cemetery, even a guardian of sorts, that comforted a young girl who was lost? Certainly not Gwen; she'd had too much experience with her exuberant, headstrong niece!

Although it was only three blocks to the Riverside Diner where she was meeting Ellen for dinner, with her knees the way they were she'd have to hustle. Or in Gwen's case, it was more like a shuffle. Putting one pink foot in front of the other, she recognized her mixture of apprehension and excitement toward their pending meeting. It would be a challenging exchange but also—as always—an adventure. A rather youngish, playful smile crossed her fifty-something face as she made her slow but steady trek to the diner. Life was never dull when you were the aunt of one Ellen Sattler!

Six

Terri eased the Ford Explorer up to the curb just around the corner from the Riverside Diner. "Take my credit card, Ellen. It's our turn to buy."

"Okay, Mom," replied Ellen, and then with a grin, she added, "I'm sure this will be the magic Tuesday where Aunt Gwen finally agrees to keep her wallet in her purse. Before you know it, moths will start building a home in there!" Terri was looking down, organizing the props in her yoga bag, grumbling in her mind over her headstrong sister-in-law and her endless refusal to let Jack and Terri pay for these weekly dinners. A short pause as Ellen stood on the curb, passenger door propped open, before crying in exasperation, "Mom! That was supposed to be a joke!"

At last, Ellen's words sunk in and Terri met her daughter's eager eyes. She allowed herself a soft chuckle and Ellen joined in. "You're right, sweetheart. Your aunt Gwen is not going to change anytime soon. She is truly choosing to bless us, and I need to just graciously accept."

"Huh, guess there's hope for you yet," Ellen said teasingly. "Have a good class, Mom!" She closed the car door and took a quick skip toward the diner before her mom could respond.

A dark-green awning stretched its provision of shade over the sidewalk. The words RIVERSIDE DINER stood in bold letters across the window's immaculately clean glass. A single bell tinkled its dutiful warning as Ellen opened the door and strolled in, her eyes scanning the small diner for her dinner companion.

One elderly couple ate in silent contentment at a table near the window. The only other customer was Gwen, sitting unsurprisingly in their usual spot. She was waving her hand at Ellen with the animated fashion you might expect of someone attempting to gain attention in a crowded banquet hall.

The young girl learned long ago not to be embarrassed; that was just Gwen. Yet noticing the odd stares from the other two patrons, Ellen chose to move quickly to the table and slide into the chair next to her aunt.

"So what are we having today?" Gwen asked.

The two looked at each other with joyful amusement in their eyes before they burst out laughing. In the five plus years they'd been having their weekly rendezvous, neither had vied from their usual "breakfast for dinner" orders. For Gwen it was two eggs over easy with dry rye toast, hash browns, and black coffee—regular. No wimpy decaf for this lady, who laughs in the face of sleeplessness! Ellen's usual was simpler: two blueberry pancakes with syrup and a large glass of skim milk.

A plump forty-something Hispanic woman with MARIA on her nametag made her way to the table with glasses of water. "Hola, girls," she said with her heavy Spanish accent. "Are we going to be daring today, or can I go to bed with my dear husband tonight knowing that one thing in this world is never different?"

"I suspect you and Roberto will sleep soundly tonight, my dear," Gwen said with a laugh that made her whole face light up.

"Oh, mi amiga, you have never heard my husband snore!" exclaimed Maria with a smile as she scribbled on her order pad. She moved quickly toward the window to check on the couple who were now done eating and gazing quietly out the window at passersby.

"So Ellen," said Gwen as she leaned in with an amused air of conspiracy, "shall we talk about Esterlynn?"

Ellen's beautiful brown eyes revealed a split second of shock before she visibly got hold of herself, reaching for her water and taking several exaggerated swigs before setting it down in the exact ring of condensation from which she'd lifted it. "Actually," she said in a conniving tone, "I was hoping we could talk about Muriel." Straightening her petite frame, she looked without wavering into the eyes of her puzzled aunt.

Gwen broke eye contact and looked around as if searching for some long-lost object. "Muriel?" she asked with confusion. "Ellen, dear, your mom told me about what happened this weekend ." She let her words fade for effect. She was hoping Ellen would decide to spill her guts about her angel encounter, more for Terri's sake really, as she'd been banking on Gwen getting to the heart of her daughter's obsession. Her eyes reconnected with her niece and she simply raised her eyebrows in a gesture of waiting.

"No, I want to talk about Muriel and her B & B up in Michigan," said Ellen with the note of finality that Gwen found all too familiar.

Maria brought their food along with a small stack of extra napkins. Sensing the intensity of the conversation, she simply said, "I'll check back with you girls in a bit."

Gwen decided to let Ellen sweat a bit. She deliberately took her time scooping her eggs onto her toast. Painstakingly, she added first salt, then pepper. Lastly, she topped the entire concoction with a healthy dose of Tabasco sauce, which Maria had knowingly provided. At last, she said, "Okay, what do you want to know about Muriel?"

Ellen jumped right in. "Well, for starters, how do you know her?"

Gwen's face reflected a woman drawing from the well of happy memories. "We met over twenty years ago when I was visiting Scotland. You wouldn't know it now, but I was quite active in my late twenties. I had always dreamed of seeing Scotland, and after several failed attempts to find a job after college, I sensed God was telling me to do some traveling first, get-my-head-cleared kinda thing." She paused to take a couple of bites of food. Ellen looked down at her own plate, waiting with feigned patience.

Gwen wiped her mouth with her napkin and continued. "I really had no interest in the big cities like Glasgow or Edinburgh, although they surely had a lot to offer with all their rich history," she said slowly. "No, I wanted to see the countryside—and not by car. I chose to hike. My favorite place was Ben Nevis. Did you know that's where *Brave Heart* was filmed?" Ellen had never heard of *Brave Heart* but nodded, fearing her aunt might get off topic. "Anyway, I stumbled upon this quaint B & B nestled near Loch Linnhe in the town of Fort William. And that, my young one, is where I first met Muriel McKenzie. She and her husband managed the B & B there in Scotland; that was almost ten years before they bought their own here in the States."

Ellen decided to cut short the history lesson, bluntly moving forward to reveal her true motive in addressing this topic and firing off her next question. "Do you think I could see it? You know, visit her up north at her B & B?"

Gwen scanned the face of the beautiful young Chinese girl for several seconds, finally deciding to answer the girl's question with her own. "Tell me: why this sudden interest in B & B's and my friend Muriel?"

Ellen's abruptly vague answer didn't really answer anything. "I've just been thinking I'd like to go up north."

It wasn't until then that Gwen noticed Ellen hadn't touched her pancakes. With a new level of concern, the older woman sent up her own question, this one to God: *Dear Lord, what's going on with this girl?*

Later that night, Ellen lay in her bed, wide-awake with her dragonfly nightlight casting just enough light to reveal a faint trace of the birthmark on her face. She ran her fingers over it lightly, a habit she'd picked up at a young age. As with most habits, one she was not aware she was doing. The remainder of their visit at the diner had been uncharacteristically quiet. She felt somewhat guilty that she'd caused Aunt Gwen to worry; she usually shared her deepest fears and desires with the wise woman because she'd earned Ellen's trust. But this time, it was different, or maybe it was Ellen who was different since her encounter with Esterlynn. She'd never felt so safe and unafraid as she had that night in the cemetery. In all her wonderings about who she really was, no *person* had ever filled her with that sort of peace before.

A slight breeze rippled the curtains of her upstairs bedroom window, drawing her from bed to sit in her favorite place at the window. It was low enough she could kneel in front of it and still see out into the yard. But Ellen rarely looked down into the yard; instead, she looked up, searching the sky. Tonight she was thinking about her birth mom. It was cloudy so there wasn't really anything to see, but it didn't really matter as her mind was far away. Sometime in the past couple of days, a seed had been planted, a general "knowing" of sorts that was growing to a point of refusing to be ignored.

Ellen closed her eyes and let the warm night breeze run its fingers through her nearly shoulder-length hair. She breathed deeply, scrunching her eyes even tighter as she used to do when she was very little, telling herself if she tried hard enough she'd be able to see the face of her birth mom. At last, she opened them, scanning the lawn below, praying for a glimpse of Esterlynn but receiving none.

All she could do now was hope that her parents would agree to let her visit the B & B after school was out in just a couple of weeks. With all the knowledge and assurance of a young girl on a predestined journey, Ellen whispered into the night, "I will find my birth mother; she's the only one that will understand."

Ellen peeled herself from the window and made her way back to bed. Dreams of heading north, even to China, filled her head that night.

Seven

Jack Sattler had a window seat on his United flight from LA to Green Bay (via Chicago). He gazed sightlessly at the tarmac as he hastened to finish the phone call before the announcement was made to turn off all cell phones and electronic devices for takeoff.

He suppressed a worried sigh as he said, "Okay, Terri, if you think this is the best thing for Ellen right now, I can be onboard with allowing this trip to St. Ignace. But I do have to go, hon. I'll be home before you know it. I love you." He touched *end call* on the touch screen of his phone and leaned back in his seat.

It had been a rough week for Jack, the first half hectic with the usual work issues and deadlines hanging over him, coupled with Terri's frantic call on Wednesday. He sighed aloud this time, rubbing the base of his neck. If his wife didn't have a history of being strong and reliable, Jack might be inclined to think she was overreacting. In the end, it was Ellen's unpredictable nature that made the whole story all too plausible.

Brynn had always been such an easy child. Even now as a teen, he and Terri had no complaints. Good grades, no serious boyfriends, content to hang around home for the most part. And then there was Ellen. She was a sweet girl, extremely intelligent and generally obedient. But there seemed to be something missing, a vacancy that often haunted her eyes. Jack and Terri had been warned about possible attachment disorder issues that many adopted families face, especially with children that have been abandoned and are left without answers to questions about their birth moms. They'd run through the gamut of reassurances, their greatest emphasis on the fact that her birth mom had chosen life for Ellen and given her away in hopes of being adopted by loving parents. Yet that hunger remained for their little girl, the tension between needing to know and knowing you never will. It could be heartbreaking at times to be the parent, wanting to have all the answers and satisfy those deep yearnings.

Having a few hours to pray and reflect on the flight home, Jack closed his eyes and allowed himself to travel back in time, reviewing the details of the adoption and that first day when Ellen was introduced to their family.

It was about twelve years ago when the couple had received news from the doctor that they could not have more children. Jack had experience with God-ordained decisions that seemed at first impossible to live with. Gwen was the older sister to Jack and his twin brother, Jeremy. Tragically, their family lost Jeremy when he was struck down and killed in front of his own home by a drunk driver at the tender age of five. The medics were able to salvage his heart, which lived on in the life of a seven-year-old recipient, now a grown woman with a husband and family of her own. This was the message of hope that Jack attempted to pass on to Terri, the idea that they had been blessed with one healthy child in Brynn and to see this as an opportunity to give a child that was already born a chance at a good life with a loving family through adoption.

After a time of grieving and soul-searching, Terri agreed to go forward with Jack's idea and they proceeded to meet with a local Christian adoption agency. After gathering data and factoring in their ages (China revering older adoptive parents and Jack and Terri being in their mid-thirties at that time), they realized their best hope of adopting an infant was to apply through an international agency working with China.

It took over a year to compile all the necessary documents for the dossier, not to mention interviews with the social worker and the required adoptive parenting classes. And so it was, nearly two years after that first meeting with the social worker, that Jack and Terri received their referral from China. The information they were given was minimal. Ellen (named at that time by the orphanage upon admittance as Xi Fu Ge) was pronounced healthy at approximately ten months old. This was based on the estimation that she was merely one week old upon her abandonment at a local police station. There was no biological history as both birth parents were unknown. The orphanage reported her as a happy baby and enclosed a small picture of an exceedingly bright-eyed Chinese girl. Their first glimpse revealed a rather sad display of a shaved head, most likely a health standard to minimize head lice throughout the orphanage.

And so it was that Jack and Terri made arrangements for Brynn to stay with her grandparents for the duration of the trip to China that would take just over two weeks. Much of that time was spent waiting for the required visa to bring the child into the United States.

Jack thought back to the incredible meeting at the airport that day in early December. Brynn, just short of seven at that time, stood at a distance at first, not sure what to make of this black-haired baby with oddly shaped, deep-brown eyes. With gentle prodding from her parents, she scuffled forward, eyes never leaving the face of her new baby sister.

Terri did her best to sound casual. "Hey, Brynn, this is her. Your new sister Ellen. What do you think?"

And with the perfect innocence of an almost seven-year-old, Brynn pointed to the side of Ellen's face and said with a loud voice, "What's *that?*"

Jack smiled now at the memory. Ellen had been born with a birthmark that was a medium brown in contrast to the rest of her rather fair skin. It started at the side of her right ear, wandering down her cheek, descending her neck, and ending its imperfect journey near her right collarbone. But oh, she was a beautiful girl. And when Ellen was old enough to ask for herself about that birthmark, Terri paused for only a moment before answering, "You know, Ellen, I just think God loved you so much he didn't want to let go of you." She touched Ellen's cheek and neck area gently. "I believe this is where God kissed you before letting you come down here to earth to be with us."

Back in the present, the flight attendant—a pretty, little, blonde thing—asked Jack what he wanted to drink. He thanked her for his coffee with cream and sugar but left it absently on the serving tray.

"Dear Lord," he prayed, "be with Terri and me as we follow your leading. Give us wisdom to know what's best for Ellen. Keep her safe and give her the peace that comes only from you."

The airline cup went untouched as Jack nodded off into an exhausted sleep. The flight would be landing soon and God was good to give Jack the rest he needed from the week gone and the one to come.

Eight

Jack and Ellen were bowling their last frame at the Super Bowl. There'd been a considerable amount of laughing and heckling on their lane; in contrast, the remaining lanes were relatively empty, since league season didn't start up again until fall. School was out now and Jack had decided to fall back on their traditional way of connecting before Gwen took Ellen up to St. Ignace—just two days from now.

Hoisting his ball from the return, Jack eyed the pins with the intensity of a surgeon preparing for open-heart surgery. He brought his arm back, made his graceful approach to the line, and released the ball. A low rumble, rumble, rumble and then the *crack* as the ball hit its mark, all but shattering the pins in a perfect strike. "Now *that's* what I'm *talkin'* about!" He punctuated this with a classic air-pumping fist.

Ellen never ceased to be amazed at how simple her dad made this game look. "It must get tiresome, getting so many strikes," she said with a tone of boredom that didn't match the excitement in her eyes. She never grew tired of seeing her dad smash those pins with the ball he'd been using since his college days.

"Perfection can be a lonely road to walk, no doubt," he said with a wink as he threw his next ball, the show of pride draining from his face as he left a two-pin split. He managed to redeem himself somewhat by picking up the split and ending with a strong score of 268.

Ellen approached the tenth frame without much hope of breaking one hundred. Her first ball hugged the gutter all the way down the left side before managing to take out one lonely pin. Her second ball surprised both of them as she recovered to pick up the spare. She looked nervously at Jack. She had a keen mind for numbers and knew she needed the miracle of a strike to close out the game with a precious score of 101. "Any advice?" she asked the master.

"I guess a quick prayer couldn't hurt," he said as he grinned.

Ellen turned slowly toward the ten pins that mocked her and reminded her of all the times she'd never quite broken one hundred. She closed her eyes and prayed a simply childlike prayer. A strange sense of hope came over Ellen as she opened her eyes. Even the pins seemed different, as if they were cheering her on!

"You can do this, Ellen," her dad said with all the love and encouragement of a devoted father.

They both held their breath as the ball made its brutally slow journey down the alley before connecting with the front pins. Slowly they began to tumble, until one remained, wobbling back and forth with indecision until at long last making its bed with the other nine.

Long arms wrapped around Ellen and swung her around in jubilant celebration. "You did it, honey! You did it! I'm so proud of you!"

Ellen giggled for the first time in weeks, allowing herself to be a little girl again. She was indeed excited about her score but more so just reveling in the love and encouragement from her father.

They made their way to the bar area, where Jack ordered a pitcher of Pepsi and a basket of bottomless fries. It was only three in the afternoon but the beer was flowing as groups of people watched the Brewers play baseball; empty pitchers were swiftly replaced with refills as the cheering grew louder.

The typical Midwest scene didn't shock Jack and Ellen; they just talked louder. Their banter was light, a lot of exaggerated bowling memories and playful arguments over past scores. The bartender brought their order just as the Brewers got a run, the group of spectators roaring their approval.

Jack's tone took on a more serious note. "I sure am going to miss you, Cookie," he said, using the pet name he'd given her as a toddler. "It seems like I'm gone so much and now you'll be up north for a good part of the summer."

A cloud of sadness brushed her face as she started mopping up ketchup with her fries. She didn't trust herself with words—how could she when she didn't know how long she'd be gone? How long did it take to get to China, and how much longer to find her birth mom? For the first time since making her decision, Ellen felt those evil cousins, fear and doubt, creeping in.

Jack, unsure how to handle her silence, decided to switch gears. "You know, I stopped there the other day, just to check it out."

"Stopped where?" asked Ellen as she took a sip of Pepsi.

"The cemetery, where you saw Esterlynn. I suppose I wanted to see if she would visit me like she did you." His eyes connected with his daughter's, a look of pleading hidden there, willing her to let him in.

"Did she? Visit you, I mean?" was Ellen's clipped response. Another loud rumble from the baseball fans allowed Jack a moment to think.

"No, she didn't." Jack paused again. "But she came to you, didn't she, Cookie?"

A flush of anger rose in her cheeks as she shouted over the noise. "Does it matter?" This conversation was sucking out all the fun and lightness of the afternoon, as far as Ellen was concerned.

"Ellen, I know you feel cheated, like no one believes you. I can understand why that would make you angry, but honey, I think God has something he wants me to say to you regardless of all that."

At this Ellen's face softened a bit; she knew her dad to be a very wise man, and if God had a message for her before she left on her journey, she figured she'd best listen up. Still fighting a sense of uncertainty, she turned to Jack and consented with two simple words. "Tell me."

It looked to be another sleepless night as Ellen rolled her father's words round and round in her mind, wondering how to move them to her heart. Gwen had told her once that this was the very essence of transition from theory to faith. Staring now at the ceiling, she strained to recall the conversation at the bowling alley.

Turning his chair to ensure direct eye contact, Jack had reached over to cover her soft, young hand with his own warm and seasoned mitt. He paused as if drawing from a source outside of himself.

"Ellen, honey," he began slowly before halting again. She knew enough about her dad to know that he was trying to hear from God; he closed his eyes, waiting for the Holy Spirit to grant the words. His lids lifted and his gaze was firm as he went on with a sense of certainty. "I know how much you struggle to comprehend God's love for you; your heart wants to believe, but your mind feels betrayed because you were abandoned. There are some things we will never understand this side of heaven, but God knows everything, and he understands your pain and confusion."

Ellen had waited at this point as her dad gave her an opportunity to jump in—to agree or disagree most likely, but she remained without words. He took this as an indication to proceed, his hand and gaze never leaving hers. "I can't help but wonder if

God sent this angel to you as a sign, a way of reassuring you that he is real and he cares for you more than you could ever know. Your mom and I have told you many times that God has a special plan for your life, but you need to believe that too, Cookie."

At this pause, Ellen did pose a question. "Is this what God wanted you to tell me, Daddy?" Her eyes were so full of adoration and assurance of whatever he might say that Jack felt a momentary sense of intimidation.

"I believe God wants you to be prepared for something. I don't know what it is specifically, only that you should be on the watch. And Ellen, you need to accept that you may or may not see Esterlynn again. God blessed you with her visit, but you need to know that no angel is higher or greater than God himself. Be very careful that you are putting your faith in God above anything else."

Later now in her bed, Ellen rolled over, snuggling deeper under the covers but with eyes still open. Many adults had scoffed at her parents for "speaking over her head" on such matters as this, but Ellen was an exceptionally mature child for her age; it was this very fact that had caused her dad to trust her with this information. The thing tormenting Ellen now was trying to decide if this changed anything. She supposed she should just stay put, pray, and trust God for answers, yet her dad said God wanted her to be prepared. Maybe this was God's way of telling her to go ahead with her plans to search for her birth mom?

Her lids were finally gaining weight as she whispered her own prayer into the dark and quiet night. "God, if it's not your will for me to see Esterlynn again, I pray you will help me be okay with that. But God, I just have to take this journey. I hope you understand and I hope you will come with me." A soft sob escaped as a single tear traveled down her cheek before adding her heart's desperate cry. "God, I need you!"

Nine

It was only 10:00 a.m. when Gwen and Ellen took the northbound ramp to US Highway 41. Already the temperature was creeping up well into the low nineties, with the humidity level so high you could almost feel a layer of moisture coating the inside of your lungs.

Jack had left for LA again Sunday night, leaving Terri and Brynn on sendoff duty. Even though it was the first week of summer vacation, Brynn was already busying herself with decisions on which AP classes to take in the fall. She seemed sincerely excited for Ellen and even made a secret visit to her sister's bedroom to give her some extra cash. "I hear they have tons of shops on Mackinac Island, not to mention *the best* fudge," she said. Even as she tried to protest, Brynn pressed a small wad of folded bills into Ellen's hand, giving her a quick kiss on the forehead and turning to leave. But not before Ellen saw the glisten of tears in her big sister's eyes.

Terri had moved about in a more common-sense fashion, checking and rechecking Ellen's packing job. Did she have enough underwear? Did she remember sunscreen? Where was her toothbrush? Would two swimsuits be enough? In fact, if Gwen hadn't shown up, Ellen would surely have ended up on an all-day let's-see-how-long-we-can-stall-this shopping spree.

"Terri, dear, we need to get going," Gwen said. "I want to try and stay ahead of the weather they're predicting." Ellen gave her aunt a lopsided grin as Terri was forced to abandon her tenth recitation of the rules for her baby girl's first extended time away from Mom.

"Are we really in for a storm?" Ellen asked now as she faced her aunt. Gwen was decked out in a bright, flowered blouse, floppy, pink canvas hat, and equally obnoxious flamingo earrings. Her hands remained at ten and two on the wheel as she turned toward Ellen, a conspiratorial grin on her face as she said, "We just never really know now, do we?"

A full-bellied laugh from Gwen lightened the mood and Ellen found herself joining in as she sat back in her seat and relaxed for the first time that day.

But the joke was on them about an hour later as they left Wisconsin and drove through Menominee, Michigan. Dark, summer storm clouds were forming in the west. Once through Escanaba, Gwen was hoping they might stay ahead of the storm as they headed east on US 2 toward Manistique, but the wind had picked up and cars were turning on their headlights as the first huge drops of rain began to smack the windshield. Small, pea-sized hail started to make its sharp pinging sounds against the car as the rain increased to bucket proportions. Gwen visibly tensed as the wipers whipped back and forth, attempting to keep up their impossible task of clearing her vision. Within seconds, she could barely make out the taillights of the car ahead of her. Confusion ensued as people started attempting to pull over. Gwen whispered a quick prayer, fearing they might be rear-ended, as she signaled near an overpass and slowed the car to a stop.

They sat in silence for a moment as lines of cars in both directions waited for the worst to pass. Ellen gazed anxiously ahead as the rain let up slightly and the wipers allowed some visibility. Wait! Did she see something?

Squinting toward the semi-protected area under the overpass, she cried, "Aunt Gwen, is that a person?" And as the rain lightened to a manageable level, Gwen saw it too. Drivers began pulling cautiously back onto the highway; the huddled figure was a safe enough distance from the road but too far away for Gwen and Ellen to make out any details. Instead of pulling back into traffic, Gwen had a clear shot now to creep forward along the shoulder and stop just short of the overpass. She turned her hazard lights on and assessed the form of a man in unseasonably heavy clothes, hat pulled low, apparently carless.

"Ellen, listen to me very carefully. You need to stay here. I'm sure he's harmless, but I would never forgive myself if something happened to you."

"But what about you?" Ellen's voice escalated as she looked worriedly at her aunt.

"The Lord will protect me," she said. But when Gwen saw the look on her niece's face, she added what she hoped to be a classic Gwen quip of assurance. "Besides, look at me!" She laughed before adding, "I may not be able to convince him with confidence, but I can sure blind him with my fashion sense!" Then suddenly, she was out of the car and hitting the lock button on her remote before Ellen could protest. The soft thud of the power locks left Ellen alone, feeling like a helplessly caged animal but with no room for restless pacing.

Ten

Ellen found her eyes darting back and forth in disbelief, first to the headrest in front of her with a mere tuft of Aunt Gwen's hair visible and then back to the man sitting shotgun in the seat Ellen herself had occupied only minutes before.

Ellen had watched the brief exchange between her aunt and the man sheltered beneath the overpass. It would have been comical the way Gwen waddled back down the slick slope with stranger in tow, if indeed the whole idea hadn't been so absurd! Was she nuts? What would her parents think? But any immediate discussion was tabled as Aunt Gwen hurriedly instructed Ellen to move to the back seat to make room for "Chuck," who needed a ride to Manistique.

The rain had stopped and a brilliant rainbow cast its colorful palette across the sky. Normally, Ellen was infatuated by rainbows, but all of her attention was drawn to Chuck. He craned his neck to take a look at Ellen, who was trying her best to look small and remain unnoticed.

"Hey there, young one, what's yer name?" he asked.

"Ellen," she said, and then added, "sir," as he looked to be in his early sixties at least. She could only see the left side of his unshaven face but still caught his startled look beneath the lowered brim of his worn leather cap with its Harley Davidson logo across the front.

As often happened, her curiosity overrode her caution as she leaned forward, straining into the seatbelt. "What? What is it?" she asked.

A loud silence hung in the air for a minute and Ellen saw Gwen steal a quick glance in Chuck's direction. His strong but narrow shoulders rose and fell as he breathed a heavy sigh, his gaze fixed on the road ahead of them. "Ellen was my wife's name." The words hung in the air with nowhere to go.

Gwen came to the rescue, breaking the awkward silence, as she explained that Ellen was her niece and they were traveling to St. Ignace from the Fox Valley in Wisconsin. She chatted on like a chickadee for several moments before reaching over to give Chuck's hand a quick pat and adding, "Me and Ellen here, we're good listeners if you were wanting to share with us about *your* Ellen."

Perhaps it was Gwen's kind nature or simply the need to tell a long-overdue story. Whatever it was, Chuck decided to trust this chattering woman and her Chinese niece.

He told about growing up in one of the poorer parts of Detroit, Michigan, his dad dying before Chuck was even five years old. His mom worked at a small auto parts manufacturing company for hours on end to support Chuck and his two younger sisters. He was only fifteen when he dropped out of high school to work at a gas station across town, sweeping floors and taking out trash for minimum wage. His mom died shortly after that and his two younger sisters ended up moving to Indiana to live with his mom's sister and her husband. Chuck was in his early twenties when he landed a job for himself at the very same auto parts company where his mom had worked. It happened within a year of his working there, on a day like any other day. He'd been walking home to his studio apartment, glancing in the window of the local diner he passed to and from work. With no money to spare, he'd never considered stopping for even a cup of coffee—until that day. *That* day he saw *her* in the window.

Again, from where Ellen was seated, it was difficult to see the expression on Chuck's face as he told his story. But sometimes understanding comes more from the tone of someone's voice than anything, and Chuck's tone shifted when he began talking about his Ellen; every recollection was laced with a deep sense of respect and admiration. She listened intently as he told of their meeting and courtship, the attraction and connection they'd had from the beginning and how sometimes you really do *just know* when you meet the right person. They were married for thirty-eight years before Ellen was diagnosed with cancer. She fought valiantly for almost three years before finally passing to the next world.

Ellen waited for what seemed an eternity, sensing she was supposed to let Chuck's story linger for a moment out of respect for his authenticity and his loss. So when he pulled a tattered and extremely used hankie from his pocket to dab his nose, Ellen saw it as a cue to jump in. "What about kids?" she asked. "Did you and Ellen have any kids?"

"Nope," he replied. "Always wanted 'em but wasn't God's plan as we saw it."

Gwen glanced in the rearview mirror in time to see the shadow cross Ellen's face, obviously not liking Chuck's matter-of-fact approach to the subject. "I'm sure," said Gwen, "God blessed you in many other ways."

A soft snort of confirmation escaped as Chuck nodded. "My Ellen loved kids and the mere fact of not havin' any to call our own wasn't gonna stop 'er from blessin' someone else's. She was always findin' ways to reach out and help other moms in our neighborhood: carin' for the little ones when the parents couldn't be home, sewin' clothes for 'em when money was hard to come by, helpin' tutor 'em with their readin' and math facts." There was a pause as Chuck pondered these things then closed the subject by saying, "Nope, our home was never lackin' when it came to lovin' on God's wee ones."

"She sounds like an amazing woman," Gwen said, wiping her own eyes with the back of her hand before reaching for her turn signal, announcing their exit from the freeway. The tension in Gwen's shoulders from driving coupled with the emotion layered in the air lent to the idea of making a pit stop. Manistique was the last town big enough to have a few options for a mid-afternoon lunch, and something told her it wasn't quite time to ask Chuck about his specific destination here in town. She glanced at the man who was much less a stranger now and asked, "Are you hungry, Chuck?"

"As a bear!" He laughed loudly before seeming to remember his manners and adding politely, "I mean, yes, ma'am. I could indeed use a bite."

Eleven

Jack sat at the desk in his hotel room in LA. He leaned back in the chair, absently clicking the save icon of the file competing for his attention on the laptop in front of him. With his cell phone pressed to his ear, he finally reached forward and hinged the monitor closed so he could focus on what Terri was saying.

He frowned deeply, trying to imagine what he was hearing. "You're saying my sister picked up a bum in Upper Michigan?"

"No, not exactly a bum," said Terri, clearly distraught over the story Gwen had relayed on the phone. "Between jobs is more the way he's describing himself from the sounds of it, but either way Jack—" A loud, exasperated groan filled his ear. He was too familiar with that groan. It spoke volumes, mostly implying, "Fix this!"

"Honey, I know Gwen is a bit unpredictable and certainly too trusting at times, but God has also given her a healthy dose of common sense. I'm sure she would not have picked this guy up if she thought there was even a hint of a chance that he was a danger to Ellen or herself."

"Common sense?" she practically yelled. "Any common sense God gave her just flew out the window the minute she got out of that car, let alone offered him a ride! I just knew this trip was a mistake! Ellen is too young to be away for this long and your sister is just too unpredictable to depend on!"

Jack had been in this marriage long enough to recognize when he needed a different approach. "Where exactly are they right now, Terri?"

"At a truck stop in Manistique. Gwen called me when he went to the restroom, this—this—Chuck fellow! I was telling her she should take Ellen and get out before he came back to the table. Wouldn't you know, at that exact moment, he *did* come back to the table? Then she calmly tells me she has to go because they're ready to order their food!"

Jack put his hand over his mouth to stifle the laugh that threatened escape as he imagined this exchange. He knew his wife and his sister very well and there would be no middle ground on this one. Quite frankly, he himself had been shocked when Terri had agreed to this whole trip to Michigan; his wife was far too practical for such an arrangement. However, he was glad she had agreed and knew it would prove to be another opportunity for Terri to let go of her control issues; he just never would have imagined she would be so challenged before they even made it to St. Ignace!

He managed to calm her down to a point where she would be able to breathe normally. As it turned out, Gwen had promised to call again before they left the diner, which couldn't be all that long. "I know you don't want to hear this, Terri, but I believe God may be testing you in this. Who are you going to trust in these minutes while you wait for that call?"

Silence on the other end. Jack held his ground and waited, praying God would be able to break past Terri's fear and speak truth to her heart. "Okay," she said at last, "but I don't have to like it."

They concluded their conversation, Terri promising to call Jack as soon as she had any information. She let out a deep sigh, and knowing Brynn was at the library, she allowed herself to call out loud to the empty house. "Lord, why does my husband always have to be so *right*?" And then, with more respect and humility, she exclaimed, "Lord, help me pass this test. You know how big this one is for me!"

Twelve

The unlikely travel trio sat around the table with its piles of soiled napkins and food baskets—the classic red plastic ones. Not a single scrap of food was left to betray their binge of burgers, fries, and onion rings. In fact, the only sign of their healthy indiscretion was evidenced by the tall metal malt mixers abandoned in their private pools of condensation.

During their session of indulgence, the conversation had surprisingly turned to talk of angels. Chuck had been the one to instigate the topic, with Ellen giving Gwen a suspicious glance every now and then. Gwen simply raised a shoulder in a subtle half-shrug as if to say, *"When could I have possibly told him your story?"*

"Makes sense if ya think about it," Chuck was saying. "With all the ways man has come up with to travel around the world, God would have to have more angels on protection duty, so to speak."

Ellen stirred the dregs of malt in the bottom of her glass, taking every precaution not to make eye contact. "So you think angels still appear to people today, like they did back in Bible times?"

Chuck rubbed his hand thoughtfully along the scruff of his bearded chin. "Well, my Ellen was more up on her Bible than I ever was, but I seem to remember a verse about talkin' to strangers and how ya never know when you might be entertainin' one. An angel, that is."

It was Gwen's turn to send a questioning look in Ellen's direction, as if to say, *"Why not tell him?"* But Ellen set her jaw firmly as she made a slow shake of her head from side to side.

Chuck gave a solid shake of his own head in the fashion of a human Etch A Sketch, clearing a memory or thought from his mind. "Well, I surely do thank ya, ma'am, for the food, but I know the two of you have a drive ahead of ya and I have my own places to go."

"Where are you going?" Ellen asked bluntly.

"Oh, I'm guessin' it'll be obvious eventually. Now you two ladies best get goin' before another batch of weather comes through."

Gwen stood as instructed, gathered her purse, and looked at Ellen as if this were the most normal thing in the world to leave this man sit here: no job, no money no plans whatsoever that she could see. Ellen didn't budge one bit. She needed to talk some sense into one of these adults, and knowing Gwen the way she did, she figured her odds to be much better with Chuck. "Who's going to take care of you?" she asked in earnest.

He turned his chair and looked full into Ellen's eyes as he leaned in and said with a wink, "The Lord will provide. He always does." And then he surprised her by digging into his jacket pocket and pulling out something tiny and gold. Ever so gently, he took Ellen's small hand and turned it, placing the object in the natural bowl-like curve of her palm. Their eyes stayed connected for several seconds, both parties scarcely breathing, until Ellen finally looked down at her upturned hand. It was a pin, a very small yet intricate pin, of a beautiful angel.

"That pin belonged to my Ellen. I know she would want you to have it. I believe everyone should have at least one angel of their own."

"Thank you," Ellen managed to whisper. Her eyes filled with tears as she threw her arms quite recklessly around this stranger; she'd known him such a short time, yet he'd found a window into her heart.

Gwen made an attempt to give Chuck some money, which he humbly declined. "Don't believe in the old belt-and-suspenders theory m'self," he said.

"Now what would that be?" Gwen asked with amusement dancing in her eyes.

"People walkin' around talkin' about believin' God will provide—that's the belt part. But they pack away bunches of money and such, disguisin' their actions under words like *investing* or *saving*. That's where the suspenders come in; the backup plan for so-called believers who aren't really trustin' in God at all. They're afraid the belt just might break."

Gwen remained silent for a moment, reveling in this man's wisdom. "Thank you, Chuck," she finally said. "You've given us way more than we've given you today." The younger girl had found her feet at some point and Gwen's arm wrapped itself gently around Ellen's shoulders as they headed toward the exit.

Chuck watched the departure of the gaudy, pink hat from his place at the table. Hot, humid air forced a greedy entrance into the air-conditioned space as Gwen held the door open in pause. She turned enough to toss one last verbal over her shoulder. "Hebrews, chapter 13, verse 2," she said, giving Chuck her warmest smile before the door shut behind them.

He stared at the closed door for a moment; an advertisement for the upcoming county fair was tacked there, crooked and slightly torn. He suspected it would be there weeks after the fair was over; it was just that sorta joint. He grinned as he stood and began collecting the table's debris as best he could into a manageable pile for the waitress.

Hebrews 13:2, the verse about entertaining angels. “I’ll be needin’ to write that one down,” he was saying to himself as his gaze landed on the bag next to Ellen’s chair. He picked it up and examined it; handmade, blue and purple quilted fabric. A small, white patch in the corner sported her name in elegant embroidery. He rushed out the door, holding the precious bag tightly by its handles, but he was too late—Gwen’s car was nowhere in sight.

Thirteen

Muriel tipped her head, trying to wipe her sweaty forehead on her upper arm, to no avail since her bare arm was equally sweaty. Carrying a bulky box down a flight of stairs made her attempt not just unmanageable but downright dangerous. Her husband, Ivan, had gone over to Mackinaw City for the day to help a friend reroof his house. This had given Muriel the perfect opportunity to carry the boxes of Christmas decorations down from the attic. Ivan, like many others in St. Ignace, thought Muriel a little off her rocker when she started her Christmas in July theme a couple of years ago. She also knew he'd be mad as a hornet when he got home and found out she'd navigated those steps without any help.

She set the heavy box labeled "outdoor porch lights" on top of a growing stack of boxes in the parlor. She glanced at the age-old clock on top of the mantel; it was nearly 4:00 p.m. Gwen had called about an hour ago, giving an abbreviated version of their day's adventure. Muriel smoothed her sleeveless summer frock and reached up to scrunch her reddish-brown curls. She could bring down that last box and still have just enough time to clean herself up before they arrived.

Muriel climbed the stairs and turned left, heading to the very end of the westbound hallway; a dozen steep, rail-less steps led to the attic, which was divided into two sections. The top of the stairs revealed a windowless storage area with a faded carpet remnant for floor covering. There was no light switch, only a single bulb in the ceiling with a pull string. A low door was tucked between cartons of storage, stacks of art supplies, and discarded paintings. Muriel walked absentmindedly past the last Christmas box and to the door. She reached down, turned the knob, and allowed the door to swing open with a low and steady creak. Her eyes scanned the tiny space (she hesitated to even call it a room) where Ellen would be sleeping.

A twin-sized bed nearly filled the area, its canopy removed as the ceiling was too low to allow for such whimsy. A round, multicolored, braided rug nearly covered the scuffed hardwood floor that peaked out at the room's four corners. One low, two-drawer dresser was squeezed in just to the right of the door with an antique doily and a pretty, flowered lamp serving as the only auxiliary items in the room. Muriel had sewn simple curtains made from a bright-yellow fabric with tiny blue flowers to hang on the solitary window overlooking the side garden. She sighed even as she looked at the matching throw pillows she'd made, the yellow starkly contrasted with the plain, blue comforter on the bed. She wanted to let Ellen stay in one of the nicely furnished guest rooms off the eastbound hallway, but Gwen had been very clear about not wanting to inconvenience Muriel and Ivan, the greatest of which would be turning away a paying guest. As much as she hated to admit it, Muriel knew that would indeed be a likely scenario here in St. Ignace in the summer. People often booked over a year in advance to stay at her B & B, a much less expensive alternative to the B & B's right on Mackinac Island. A thirty-minute ferry ride was the only thing separating her guests from all the delights the island had to offer.

She wandered back out to the storage area. Perhaps she could hang one or two of her dusty, discarded paintings on the wall to cheer the space up. Back in Scotland, she'd had more time to paint. The beautiful countryside provided endless brush strokes of panoramic settings. Muriel kneeled down, fanning through the vertical stack of memories like dust-covered dominoes.

Ding-ding-ding-ding!

That couldn't be ? Muriel thought as she glanced at her wristwatch. *Oh, yes, it could be!* She pulled herself to her feet, once more dismissing the last Christmas box. A more persistent *ding-ding-ding-ding* came from the bell at the front desk as she made her way down the attic stairs.

The Scotswoman made another futile attempt to tame her curls as she passed the wall of boxes and rounded the corner. There stood her dear old friend, familiar as ever in a crazy getup with matching hat and earrings. Any other time, Muriel would have rushed in for a hearty hug, but the girl standing next to Gwen made it impossible not to pause. Her eyes filled with tears as she took in Ellen: her jet-black hair, bright eyes, and perfect skin. Her petite frame was outfitted in jean shorts and an emerald green tank top that was gathered at the chest and flared out as it rested just below her waistline.

Her gaze never left Ellen as she exclaimed, "Oh Gwen! She is indeed a beaut!"

Fourteen

It was Saturday afternoon, her fourth full day in St. Ignace. Ellen walked along the rock-strewn shore of Lake Huron, about a mile down the road from The Celtic Inn, Ivan and Muriel's B & B. She found herself pacing back and forth restlessly, looking for good skipping stones. Her dad would be proud to see how much she'd improved her technique: whizzing stones across the surface of the water, sometimes skipping as many as three times before dropping out of sight.

The trip was not going as she'd expected. The first major hitch had been her brainless error in leaving her bag behind in Manistique. She missed her diary, but the bigger problem was the money: nearly $250 altogether (totaled by a generous allowance from her mom, the under-the-table contribution from Brynn, plus her own stash). Every penny was gone. She sat on the nearest bench with heaviness quite beyond a girl of ten. What did it matter really? Had she actually believed she could get to China on a measly $250?

She looked to her left and made out the distant image of the Mackinac Bridge. The Mighty Mac was indeed impressive as the longest suspension bridge of its type in the United States, connecting upper and lower Michigan. Ellen rode across it Wednesday morning after Gwen had left for home. It was fun riding in the high cab of the Ford truck with Muriel and Uncle Ivan (she'd adopted his self-imposed dubbing, even though it never sounded quite right to her). It had been a good day; while Uncle Ivan finished his roofing job, she and Muriel had perused the shops of Mackinaw City. As the stifling humidity morphed into a light rain, the duo ducked into the bridge museum for a tour. The museum was situated on the second floor of the building with Mamma Mia's restaurant below. Here, they'd rounded off the day's experience with a large pepperoni pizza.

But now, from miles away, the bridge appeared to be a toy model, its mightiness dwindling as surely as her hope. Ellen was afraid to tell Gwen about her misplacement of funds, which left her forced to confide in her hostess. Muriel promptly offered to pay her for helping out around the B & B, the result of which found Ellen unpacking boxes of endless Christmas decorations.

The obvious question of *why* flashed off and on in her mind as they hung the outdoor lights and positioned the lighted Nativity on the perfectly maintained lawn. They moved indoors, her question mutely persisting as they draped and spiraled green garland everywhere, looking like a grand tree explosion in Ellen's eye. It wasn't until they'd decorated the lobby tree and set the last candle on the fireplace mantel that Ellen asked, in cordial terms of course, taking care not to blatantly question the woman's mental state.

Muriel laughed long and loud. "Oh dear, if I only had me a dollar for every folk that be askin' me that question!" Then, with a twinkle in her eye, she reached down and gently cupped Ellen's face with her work-worn hands. "Christmas is a season of hope, as well it should be; but one day, the Lord told me that once a year just twasn't enough for folks to be hopeful. I'm supposin' that's how it all started—my Christmas in July!"

The remainder of the day had been more like an Easter egg hunt as Muriel emptied packing peanuts and crumpled newspapers from every opened box. They'd searched in earnest for the absent angel that was conspicuously missing from the tree's top, all to no avail.

Remembering the scene brought thoughts of Esterlynn to Ellen's mind. She reached down, subconsciously caressing the angel pin, reminding her of Chuck. People talked about Christmas miracles all the time. Why not believe for a Christmas miracle in July? One thing seemed certain: it was a good time to pray. "Lord, I've sure made a mess of things here, no money and all. I feel like I'm wasting time. Am I trying to force something that wasn't meant to be? Maybe my plans aren't your plans. But Lord, you brought me here. Give me a sign. Mom always says we have not because we ask not. So I'm asking, Lord, show me why I'm here before I have to go home."

Fifteen

Ellen's walk back to the Celtic Inn took her past the dock for the Star Line Ferry that took passengers to and from Mackinac Island. She was fascinated by the forty-foot spray that projected from the back of the hydro-jet ferry. Being late June, tourism was at its peak for the summer. The line of passengers for the next incoming ferry was snaking back and forth already even as the last one was leaving the dock. From here, Ellen could see the distant island where the ferries from both St. Ignace and Mackinaw City traveled daily. She was intrigued by Mackinac Island and hoped to get a chance to visit before she left.

There were no motorized vehicles allowed on the island, save for emergency vehicles. It was a land of horse-drawn carriage rides, bicycles, shopping, and fudge. There were plenty of historical sites to visit also; the Grand Hotel (still functioning since 1887) and Fort Mackinac were among the more popular attractions. Ellen took a glance at the ticket price, comparing it to the money Muriel was paying her. The cost for the ferry alone was doable, but she would need extra cash for spending. She chided herself once more for being so careless with her money. "If I'm meant to go, it'll work itself out," she said aloud, with complete resolution.

Ellen spotted Muriel behind the desk as she walked into the air-conditioned lobby of the B & B. Her hostess was working on the computer with a furrowed brow that clouded her face every time she struggled with "these infernal technical gadgets," as

Muriel liked to call it. She was muttering something under her breath with her animated Scottish flare. Her unruly curls were pulled back from her face with a multicolored scarf, her half-glasses having slid to the very last place of purchase on the end of her nose.

When she saw Ellen, the look of frustration was immediately replaced with a broad smile that triggered a twinkle in her eyes. "You, me dear, are a sight for sore eyes. Not to mention a right proper excuse for an old woman to take a break and sip some iced tea on the back porch. Would you agree?"

Minutes later, the two were sitting on the wooden swing with its brightly colored cushions, its A-frame base built with a small canopy to bless its occupants with a reprieve from the scorching summer sun. Cobblestone paths wound their way through the beautiful flowering gardens and around the gazebo that stood between the Inn and the marshy shore of the lake. From here, again, one could see the distant outline of Mackinac Island. Muriel was relaying the history of St. Ignace and the island as they swayed gently in the swing, a warm breeze bumping against them as the ice in their tea swiftly shrunk.

Ellen loved listening to Muriel talk and had always been a big fan of any kind of history. But in that moment, she caught only bits and pieces about a mission for Huron Indians, American fur trading, and the lore of the great turtle. Her mind wandered as questions popped up with annoying persistence: Should she go ahead with her original plan to find her birth mother, even with the odds stacked against her? Would she see Esterlynn again? And perhaps the biggest question of all: could she simply let go of this whole crazy scheme, forget Esterlynn, and go back to life as it was?

Somehow, she knew it wasn't time to make that decision. The reason she had come here was not yet clear. She would trust God; she had to believe that he was going to show her the way, perhaps through the sign she'd asked for. Who knew this trip was going to be a lesson in faith and waiting on God?

Later that evening, Ellen gave a call home using her mom's cell phone from the privacy of her little attic room. (Terri's separation anxiety from her phone had proven less than her fear of Ellen traveling without one.) Luckily, Ellen hadn't left *that* in her bag at the truck stop!

Ellen was pleasantly surprised to have both of her parents on the line, her dad working from home this week. There was a tone in her mom's voice that Ellen loved to hear but seldom experienced when her dad was away. She was more relaxed, less anxious. Dare she say content? Call it what you will, the result was comforting to the young girl. She felt a connection to that contentment, even miles apart, with an uncertain path in front of her.

They chatted casually for the next half hour. Dad was busy working on several projects. Mom had taken on more hours at the yoga center as one of the teachers had quit without notice. Brynn was keeping busy with lifeguarding at the neighborhood pool and spending time with Josh whenever their schedules allowed. Ellen smiled, feeling quite safe and sure for the first time in days, until her dad asked a question that jarred her. Something, quite frankly, she'd conveniently dismissed.

"So, Cookie, tell us. Whatever became of Chuck?"

Guilt wrapped its ugly arms around Ellen as she realized she'd been so preoccupied with her missing money that she'd never given much thought to where Chuck may have ended up.

Ellen glanced out her little window, the edge of the lake still visible in the fading light of day. "I honestly don't know, Daddy."

There'd been some other talk, mostly about when Ellen might return home. The requisite love-you was exchanged with teary voices before ending the call. As Ellen plugged her phone charger into the outlet, she asked God to forgive her for dismissing Chuck so quickly from her thoughts. "Please, Lord, keep him safe in his journeys. Keep us *both* safe."

Sixteen

Chuck walked with a steady pace along the Interstate 75 Business Spur in Sault Saint Marie, Michigan. He felt that his interview at The Coffee House had gone reasonably well, and now he would just have to wait. He'd given the manager, Mrs. Sullivan, the phone number of the motel where he was staying. Chuck had learned to be upfront and honest when interviewing, no sense pretending he wasn't basically a vagabond, floating from job to job. They'd find out eventually anyway.

Walking along the bridge that crossed Saint Mary's Canal, a familiar Scripture came to mind. As he studied the water's flow, he reflected on the verse that talked about believing and not doubting when we ask God for wisdom. The one who doubts is like a wave of the sea and should not expect to receive anything. He had prayed for wisdom before coming to Sault Saint Marie; now he must believe.

He'd spent a couple of days looking for employment opportunities in Manistique, and with a population of 3,600 people, two days were enough. Chuck had concluded his search at the same truck stop where he'd last seen Gwen and Ellen, having tucked Ellen's bag carefully into the middle pocket of his bulging backpack. Madge, the waitress working the counter, came over to refill his coffee. She didn't have to ask if he'd had any luck finding a job; his contemplative demeanor spoke for itself. "Say Chuck, you might consider heading back toward Escanaba or farther north to Sault Saint Marie. Those towns each sport whopping populations between thirteen and fifteen thousand. That would broaden a man's possibilities by quite a bit, I suspect." Madge was truly a blessing, even allowing him to use her smart phone to do a bit of research. Sault Saint Marie was a college town. Lake Superior State University had about 2,500 students, Michigan's smallest private university.

Chuck thanked Madge for her help and promised to stop in again before he left town. He found himself walking along the streets of Manistique; armed with such scant data on the two towns, he knew his answer would have to come from God. He wished, as he still so often did, that his dear Ellen were here to discuss the idea. It's been said that the seasons where you're alone are the ones that allow you to really get to know God. Chuck was learning that lesson firsthand. He didn't guess he'd ever hear from God in such profound ways that Ellen had, but she had always insisted that God speaks to each person in their own language. Chuck was a simple man who felt things in his gut. That was often the closest he could come to what might be called confirmation from God. He had prayed, he had asked for wisdom, and his gut was saying he should go to Sault Saint Marie. In fact, this had been a pretty strong sense, almost a tugging at his soul. Could there be a specific purpose drawing him to that particular town? He supposed God knew, and that was enough for him. He'd hitched his way north with a truck driver. The conversation had been nowhere near as lively as his exchange with Gwen and Ellen, but the man was kind enough and had dropped him at the first gas station within the city limits. Using the clerk's directions, Chuck walked to the local library; using their Internet, he'd found out about the job opening at The Coffee House.

His time of reflection now ended as he pulled his room key from his pocket. The door of room 214 swung open to reveal the outdated bedspread and furnishings. Chuck eased his heavy pack onto the bed before turning to open the '70s style drapes: an avocado green with an ugly orange paisley swirl that resulted in a kaleidoscope of confusion. He looked out the window at the white plastic chairs angled toward each other on the balcony outside his room. The motel was clean enough and most importantly in his price range. The AC unit in the window was silent, having left it off intentionally. Somehow, no matter how hot it was, there was a closed-in feeling that accompanied the running of the AC that was too stifling for Chuck.

He left his room door open and went back outside. He watched the comings and goings of the people in the parking lot below from his plastic perch. Anyone within a few feet could have heard Chuck. In low, sweet tones, he gave his Ellen an update on the events of the past few days. The average onlooker would assume he was a little crazy perhaps, but it gave him comfort. He told his wife about the bag that little Ellen had left behind in Manistique. It had taken several attempts before he had finally allowed himself to go through its contents. He knew he was invading the girl's privacy, yet if he ever had hopes of returning it to her—? Well, he would have to see what was inside. Perhaps confiding to his deceased wife would make the whole thing less shameful. The pretty bag had surprisingly contained only three things: a small, travel-size Bible (*to Ellen from Mom and Dad at Christmas*), an as-of-yet blank journal with accompanying pen, and $250 in cash. On the inside cover of the journal, scrawled in a young-person's cursive, was the name *Ellen Sattler.* Chuck had made a vow to God that someday, someway, he would return the bag and its contents to his little friend. There was no sense trying to track her down in St. Ignace, since Gwen had implied their trip to be a short summer stay.

The whole thing had been a blessing in disguise for Chuck. The extra cash had been just enough to allow him to rent this room, at least for a few weeks until he had a regular paycheck. He thought about his explanation of the belt and suspenders that he'd shared with Gwen and Ellen. God had indeed provided. And little Ellen—less than sixty miles south of where he sat in this cheap hotel just south of Canada—how was she doing?

It was time to quit talking to his wife and resume his talk with God. "Father God, thank you for crossing my path with Ellen's. May your angels watch over Ellen in St. Ignace and keep her safe. Thanks again for your provision. Lord, I'm trusting that you will provide a way for me to return Ellen's belongings. And finally, if it be your will, I could sure use this job at The Coffee House."

Seventeen

July fourth produced a gorgeous sunny day with temps in the mid-eighties and pleasantly low humidity. Ellen had spent the afternoon helping Muriel set up for the party that she and Ivan were hosting, an annual event that included guests from the B & B and local friends, several of whom also boasted a Scottish heritage. The food would be traditional American picnic cuisine. Ellen had never seen such a spread: mounds of brats and hamburgers, pounds of potato and pasta salads, along with fresh fruit platters and corn on the cob. A separate table was set up just for desserts: cookies, brownies, lemon bars, and mini cheesecakes. And just in case that wasn't enough, they'd set aside all the fixings for s'mores to be toasted over the fire pit around sunset, just prior to the fireworks show.

The whole affair would take place in the spacious backyard. The red, white, and blue lights on the gazebo along with the patriotic tablecloths and centerpieces would be permitted to coexist with the Christmas decorations for one day. Ten round, wooden tables were set up, painted white with folding chairs to match.

Ellen set the last chair in its place. "Six chairs at each table! Sixty guests! Will you really have that many, Muriel?"

"Well, me gram always said 'tis better to have extra and send folks home with food than to send 'em home hungry. Wouldn't want that now, would we?"

Ellen smiled at Muriel in her PROUD TO BE AN AMERICAN T-shirt and dangly earrings of red, white, and blue stars. "Your gram sounds like a smart lady." She was enjoying her quirky host and felt comfortably closer to her after their chat earlier that morning.

While peeling potatoes, Ellen had surprised herself by telling Muriel about her encounter with Esterlynn. The excitement of the party juxtaposed with the fact that Ellen was scheduled to go home in a few short days may have triggered Ellen's vulnerable mood.

Muriel had listened with earnest attention as Ellen relayed her story, her right hand a blur as she skillfully skinned the potatoes into the large sink. She never once interrupted or made eye contact. She just listened, mumbling a faint "Mm-hmm" or "A-ha" every so often. Once Ellen finished, a few moments of almost sacred silence rested between them before Muriel said anything.

Ellen waited nervously, her defenses cautiously ready. Muriel, however, surprised her by never once questioning the validity of her story. Discussions about angels were apparently commonplace for this Scots woman. Or was she simply humoring a young girl's imagination? Ellen couldn't be sure. Regardless, the most interesting revelation from the conversation was still replaying itself in the back of Ellen's mind. Muriel's only observation had involved the gender of Ellen's angel. She pointed to the fact that anytime angels were referenced by gender in Scripture, it was in the masculine sense. This had indeed given Ellen pause to ponder.

It was later that evening, and the party was just past peak with the guests settling in for the fireworks display. Ellen excused herself for a bit and climbed the stairs to her attic room. Her stomach had its fill of food and her ears their fill of stories (namely the ghosts of Independence Days past). Her tired eyes caught a glimpse of the box as she crossed the small storage room to her bedroom. Could it be *another* box of Christmas decorations? Ellen eased her petite frame down next to the box and opened its dusty flaps. She cleared away the crumpled newsprint and found herself staring eye-to-eye with the famous missing angel, the lobby's tree still bare of her presence.

Something stirred deep within Ellen as she held the angel gently in her hands. She had blonde hair with blue eyes that matched her elegant dress; her wings splayed proudly behind her back. She was perfect. And suddenly, Ellen understood. Esterlynn didn't look anything like this! She wasn't some Barbie doll version of a divine messenger. Ellen closed her eyes and thought back to that night. She had never pictured Esterlynn as a female. It wasn't until Ellen had been given permission to name God's guardian that she'd attached any sort of gender reference. She supposed it was natural for a little girl to imagine that such a comforting force would have a somewhat maternal quality.

She carried the angel ever so gently into her room and sat on the edge of her bed. She had a bird's-eye-view of the party on the lawn below her. The fireworks had started and one brief reflection managed to almost light up Chuck's angel, pinned to her red, cotton shirt. There were few times in her young life when Ellen had felt a strong sense of God's presence. This would forever be one of those moments; and with it, she somehow knew she would see Esterlynn again.

Of course, she had no way of knowing how very soon it would be.

Eighteen

The guests were saying their good-byes as Ellen returned to the backyard scene. Hugs and handshakes were accompanied by laughter and lighthearted farewells. Ivan and Muriel stood in mute satisfaction, his arm curved around her shoulders and hers wrapped around his waist. Whispered words, too private to share, glanced between them as Ellen looked on from a cordial distance.

Not wanting to trespass on their moment, Ellen started clearing the tables. Her hosts reluctantly loosened themselves from their romantic episode and joined in the cleanup. Ivan carried trays of leftover food into the kitchen. Muriel gathered the centerpieces while Ellen put the rest of the paper plates and discarded food into the huge trashcan.

It was nearly dark now with tiki torches burning haphazardly around the backyard. A slight curtain of smoke still rose from the fire pit as Ellen started folding chairs. Muriel came up behind her and rested her hands softly on Ellen's shoulders. "That's enough for tonight, me dear one."

"But there's so much work to do yet—." Ellen began.

"Tell you what," said Muriel. "You come to the kitchen for a tub o' soap and water to wipe down these here tables and we'll call that done. Besides, I have something for you." Ellen followed her, quite relieved that she was almost done for the day. But instead of going to the kitchen, Muriel headed to the front desk. Ellen's eyes widened as Muriel handed her two twenties and a ten.

"Now don't be lookin' at me in such a way. This be a fair wage for all you've done for me and Ivan. Your auntie Gwen'll be pickin' you up in a day or two, and we don't want her makin' this her business now, do we?"

Ellen threw her arms around the middle-aged Scottish woman. "Oh, thank you, Muriel! You have no idea how much this means to me!"

"This lady's been 'round more than you might think," Muriel said with a wink. "Now get yerself out to those tables while it's still the *Fourth* of July!"

Ellen said a quick prayer of thanks as she tucked the cash deep down into the front pocket of her jean shorts; no way was she losing this too! She filled a large bucket with hot, soapy water and grabbed a couple of clean dishrags. She set the bucket on the closest table and drew in a tired breath; it wouldn't take long to wipe down the tablecloths. She needed a short break. She wandered between the tiki torches, past the gazebo, and settled onto the backless stone bench facing the lake. Scanning the distance, she was able to make out the dark shadow of Mackinac Island. She wondered if Muriel would have time to take her before she returned to Wisconsin. She wondered if she'd even *be* returning to Wisconsin.

Then, in God's perfect timing, she saw it. Just to the right of the fire pit, the same familiar glow from that night in the cemetery. She rubbed her eyes, thinking she was just tired. She looked again, but there was no mistake.

It was Esterlynn!

Even knowing she'd see her again could not have prepared her for this. She felt that same sense of reverent fear wash over her.

She had no words. She just gazed in awe as two powerful words met her ears. "It's time."

Her mind raced as she finally found her tongue. "Time for what? Oh Esterlynn, please tell me! I know that you are an angel sent from God. What does he want me to do? Where am I supposed to go?"

"Watch for a sign. Then you will know where to go. You will find the answer you seek." And then the angel was gone, the departure as sudden as the arrival.

Ellen jumped up from the bench. "Wait! What sign?" Her heart was racing as she paced frantically, hoping upon hope that Esterlynn was still there. She actually found herself looking among the rushes along the shoreline. "Get a grip, Ellen. Angels don't hide!" she chided herself. Returning to the bench, she reviewed the message. Esterlynn had said it was time and to watch for a sign. And that was exactly what she would do.

Only the faith of a child could have been so effective. She curled up on the bench, in much the same fashion she'd been on the ground that night in the cemetery. And she watched.

Minutes or hours may have passed. Finally, a bright arc of reddish light crept into view just over the island. This got her attention and she stood up. Were the fireworks starting again? No, it was a continual brightness and it was growing. She staggered to the shoreline, hoping to discern what she was seeing. The light was big and bright and rising. Unbelievably, it was the moon! And as it gained height over the island, it cast a bright reflection onto the water. The higher it rose, the farther its path of light stretched. Brilliant fingers extended to meet Ellen's feet at the water's edge, as though the island beckoned her.

This was it! This was the sign! It had to be. One way or another, Ellen Sattler was going to Mackinac Island—tomorrow.

Nineteen

Ellen was grappling with two opposing feelings inside of her: excitement and guilt. The excitement rose from the fact that she was on her way to Mackinac Island. She smiled and squinted into the sun from her seat on the top deck, loving the wind as it whipped through her short bob of hair. The ferry was quite full, having caught the popular 9:00 a.m. departure. Her strategy had proven brilliant and effective, even if it was the very source of her guilt.

She'd surprised Muriel by showing up for breakfast at 7:00 a.m., attempting to pick up on any plans her hosts might have for the day. Ivan was gone already. With today being the last dry day in the forecast, he planned to make the most of it, his sights on finishing the roofing job in Mackinaw City. Muriel would be swamped with guests checking out. Being July 5, people seemed programmed to leave their adventure behind and return to their normal lives as they knew them.

Ellen contemplated the facts, considered asking Muriel to take her to the island tomorrow, but decided she couldn't risk waiting a day. Esterlynn's words resonated in her head. Surely—*it's time*—called for immediate action! She'd asked Muriel's permission to explore the area, emphasizing the fact that she would be going home soon and time was short. Hence, her first stab of guilt was birthed in her conviction that she had not been completely honest with Muriel. Her new Scottish friend would never have approved of Ellen's plan to hop the next ferry to the island alone.

She'd purchased her ticket at the Star Line Ferry booth at the far end of the parking lot, a good distance from the dock area. She wasn't sure if the ticket takers would question a young girl taking a day trip to the island without an accompanying adult, but she knew she couldn't take the chance. So her second dance with guilt came as she wandered toward the loading zone and assumed the role of stalking tourists. With the early morning temperature already climbing, Ellen stood stealthily in the shade of a young tree, waiting for her opportunity. Her efforts were rewarded within ten minutes as a wealthy Asian couple got in line, at least six variations of luggage in tow. It was difficult to discern if they were actually Chinese from this distance, but Ellen knew from experience that most Americans either couldn't or didn't take the time to try to distinguish among Asian cultures. Fortunately, in this case, it worked to her advantage as she sidled up to the couple. She stood close enough for the average onlooker to assume she was their daughter, while distant enough that the couple shouldn't notice their tagalong. The ticket taker simply smiled as she boarded, extending the usual platitudes about enjoying the island.

As the island grew closer, passengers looked in Ellen's direction, trying to catch their first glimpse of the Grand Hotel sprawled along the island's southwestern edge; even from here, you could see its tall, white columns and bright-yellow awnings along its vast wraparound porch. The ferry's jet stream diminished as they lost speed. The American flag slowed its frenzied flapping from the rear of the upper deck. Ellen could see Fort Mackinac high on the bluff as the ferry pulled smoothly up to the dock. She felt nearly giddy as she shadowed her pseudo-parents down the stairs, off the ferry, and onto the dock. She was instantly swallowed in the shuffle of unloading bikes and luggage. Even from here, at the far end of the dock, the overwhelming smell of horses wafted at her nose. Mixed with it was a sensational combination of culinary odors, causing an instinctive rumble in her stomach.

Ellen and the other passengers made their way down the long, wooden dock. People pushed bikes, carried babies, towed toddlers, and snapped pictures from their cameras or phones as they moved toward the main market area and visitors center. Everyone was in grand spirits. Ellen studied her map; now that she was actually here, she wasn't sure what to do. *Lord, where would you have me go?*

With no immediate reply, she just started walking. She found herself awed by the hustle and bustle of traffic. People traveling on foot were wise to watch for bikers, enamored by all the sights and weaving in and out among the various horse-drawn transports. Piles of horse apples peppered the streets, evidence of the island's population of four hundred horses encompassing livery carriages, horse-drawn carriage tours, drive-yourself carriages, and simple horseback riders.

Ellen had read that a person could tour the circumference of the entire island in one day's visit by bike. However, in the necessity of saving money, she chose to walk along the main street rather than renting a bike. She peeked in the windows of souvenir shops, sandwiched between tasty fudge shops and restaurants. Her map led her to Cadotte Avenue, where she found herself climbing uphill toward the Grand Hotel. Countless carriages climbed up and cruised down, loaded with passengers shaded by colorful surreys.

She marveled at the majestic hotel from her place on the sidewalk along the street. The rolling grounds and perfectly manicured hedges invited guests to linger and enjoy the spot where history and romance met. She conserved some more money by declining the tour inside the Grand Hotel. The grassy shade was inviting in the day's heat and she decided to sit for a spell before heading back downtown.

An upward carriage paused right in front of her. The driver seemed to be talking to the magnificent, sleek, black team of horses, their muscles twitching as their ears turned toward their master. There were four benches loaded with passengers, but Ellen's gaze was curiously drawn to the driver. She looked to be a young Chinese woman, possibly under twenty, her long, silky, black hair pulled back into a tail not unlike those of her equine workers. She wore a tan, derby-style hat pulled low. Her lightweight, checkered blouse was tucked neatly into her jeans. Her work boots, caked with a mud-manure combination, managed to look dainty on the young woman's tiny feet.

Strangely, the driver turned her head, almost sensing the girl, and held her eyes for several seconds. She smiled at Ellen. It was the most beautiful smile she had ever seen, lighting up her perfectly sculpted Chinese features. She returned her attention to her horses; making a clucking sound, the team strained forward. Ellen could hear a muffled version of the driver's tourist report to her passengers, undoubtedly some fun-fact trivia concerning the Grand Hotel.

No one watching Ellen in that moment could have missed the goofy smile on her face. She'd been thrilling at the sights and sounds of the island, but it wasn't until that moment—locking eyes with the carriage driver—that she'd felt a sense of connection. *Weird*, she thought. A vague memory came back to her, the story from Chinese folklore of an invisible red thread connecting their people. Her thoughts were interrupted by the audible rumble from her stomach. She snuck one last peek over her shoulder before heading back to town for lunch. The mysterious driver and carriage were nowhere in sight.

Twenty

After satisfying her hunger with a chilidog and french fries, Ellen felt reenergized and ready to explore. She traveled the main road once again, east this time, along the southern part of the island. She headed north, where Main Street became Lake Shore Boulevard, keeping a watchful eye on the multitude of distracted bicyclists. She went as far as Arch Rock, an amazing natural rock structure rising 146 feet above the water. The brochure explained that thousands of years of wind and water had eroded the soft rock below, leaving only the hard rock to form the arch, which spanned fifty feet at its widest point.

The brochure boasted of many beautiful sights to see along the road that hugged the Lake Huron shore. With a bike, she could loop up over the north end, cruise south along the western shore, and close the route back near the Grand Hotel. Unable to overlook the obvious problem of having no bike, she retraced her steps and found herself once again on the main road near the docks. She wandered into the closest fudge shop, unable to hide the bugging of her eyes as she saw the endless assortment of fine fudge flavors. She splurged and bought a sample pack that had peanut butter, mint chocolate, pistachio, and butter pecan. She found a quiet picnic area near the lake and took a tiny nibble of each piece of fudge. A good distance down the shoreline, she could see dozens of bright kites flying against the blue sky, a brilliant kaleidoscope of colors accentuated by the breathtaking aquamarine of the water below.

From just behind her, a voice said, "Amazing, aren't they?" Ellen twisted her torso to see the Chinese carriage driver, a short distance away, looking directly at her. That sense of connection completely washed over her once again. She couldn't seem to get past the reality of the woman's breathtaking beauty. But this was not a one-sided exchange; the carriage driver was staring at Ellen in a way that would have been unnerving if it hadn't seemed so natural.

Maybe it was the magic of the island or the surreality of the situation, but Ellen's question seemed to be the only one that begged asking, "Do I know you?"

The next hour found the kindred spirits sitting side by side on the grass, crisscross-applesauce, Ellen's right knee connecting with her new friend's left. Although the young woman spoke as an open book, Ellen sensed this was not her typical venue. She explained that she was working on the island for the summer and would be starting college this fall. She'd spent her senior year of high school with a nice family in Kingsford, Michigan, as a foreign exchange student. Her friends there had nicknamed her Jade—she presumed in association with the stone so common to her native China. She told stories of growing up in the countryside of Hunan province. She had a younger brother, considerably younger at only six years old. When her mother died two years ago, her father determined it wise for her to seize the opportunity for an education in America. It had been a very difficult thing for Jade, leaving her family and her country behind, basically divorcing everything she had ever known.

Jade's story flowed readily into Ellen's anxious ears. She had never been so enamored with someone she had just met. She kept stealing quick glances, studying the young woman's profile. She had a perfectly chiseled jaw, her eyelashes long and without makeup. Her mouth moved with precision as she took care in choosing each word—her tongue attempting to feign comfort with the English language.

Jade was curious about Ellen's visit to the island, specifically the notion of such a young girl coming here all alone. Ellen filled her in on most of the surface facts, intentionally implying that Ivan and Muriel had approved her trip for the day. She wanted to tell Jade about Esterlynn and the directive to come to the island but wasn't willing to risk her new friend laughing at her—or worse, simply walking away.

Jade had the rest of the day off and asked Ellen if she wanted to bike around the island. "I don't have a bike," she told Jade.

The young woman grinned, a mischievous look crossing her face. "But do you have a spirit for adventure?"

The afternoon sun beat down on them as Jade stood on her bike pedals and pumped hard. Ellen giggled like a little girl from the seat behind her, feet jutting out, arms working to keep purchase with Jade's bobbing waist. Having removed her hat and freed her long mane from its tail, Jade's long hair only heightened Ellen's laughter as it tickled her face with abandoned frenzy. Time was forgotten as the pair cycled around the entire island, stopping here and there, chatting the afternoon away. Ellen told Jade about her family and being adopted. She talked about her teacher and her best friend, Emily. She shared her deepest wonders about her birth mom and why she'd abandoned her. It wasn't until they stopped at the stables that the topic of faith was raised.

"Hey, Jerome," Jade said to the man cleaning out the stalls. A frown furrowed his brow, posing the question without use of words. "She's my sister," Jade lied. Jerome shrugged his shoulders with a low grunt of dismissal and continued with his work. She led Ellen by the hand to Gunther's stall, Jade's favorite horse. He was so massive that Ellen needed to stand on a stool just to stroke the blaze on his forehead.

"Are you always so quick to lie?" Ellen asked, feeling slightly betrayed by her newfound hero.

"Sometimes, there is a fine line between truth and untruth," Jade mused. Ellen puzzled on her response for a bit, watching as Jade groomed Gunther.

"My mom hates lies. She says God is truth and we hurt him when we deceive people."

This comment opened the door for a discussion of faith. Jade admitted that while she believed in some form of superior existence, she was not raised to believe in God as Christians professed him.

Sadness welled up in Ellen's heart. Jade was missing so much! And so it was, in her own spirit of evangelism, that Ellen wound up telling Jade about God sending her an angel—not just once but twice. They had retreated to a bench outside the stable, Jade looking steadily into the eyes of her young friend as she absorbed the details of Ellen's angelic encounters. "I believe Esterlynn sent me here," Ellen said in conclusion. "I—I—think maybe I was supposed to meet you!" she stammered, her eyes wild with excitement.

Twenty-one

It was nearly 6:00 p.m. and Muriel was pacing. She'd not given the girl a specific curfew, but surely, she should have been back by now! Ivan would be home soon, and what then? "Lord, give me wisdom. Show me what to do," she prayed. Perhaps some fresh air would help. As she made her way to the rear entrance, her ears caught the distant chirping tone of the lobby's phone. She hustled with a combination of hope and fear; in one swift motion, she stabbed the talk button and raised the phone to her ear. "Ellen?"

"Yes, Muriel, it's me."

"Lord, have mercy, young one! I was beside meself with worry! Yer cell phone up there in yer room, no way to reach ya!"

Ellen closed her eyes tightly as she told Muriel of her excursion to the island, relieved for the moment by the miles of water separating the two of them. It had been Jade's idea to call and check in with her host at the B & B, loaning Ellen her cell phone. Her new friend was giving her a questioning look as she caught the indiscernible tirade spewing from the phone's speaker. Ellen looked away, not willing to subject herself to Muriel's audible anger and Jade's visual disappointment all at once.

"Please don't, Muriel," Ellen pleaded. "I can catch the next ferry back by myself. You don't need to buy a ticket just to take me right back." A slight pause as she listened and chanced a quick glance at Jade. "All right. I will take the seven o'clock ferry and meet you at the dock in St. Ignace. I really am sorry, Muriel." She touched the screen on Jade's phone and buried her head in her hands. In an instant, the clip-clop of horse hooves had gone from melodic to thunderous. "Man, am I in trouble!" she moaned.

"It appears to me you are not the one to be lecturing on deception," Jade said sternly. But when Ellen spread her fingers to sneak a peek, Jade's face showed nothing but a bemused grin. Suddenly, both girls were laughing uncontrollably; silliness overpowered them until they were literally rolling on the ground. Jade recovered first, grabbing Ellen's hand and pulling her to a standing position. "Come on," she said. "The last thing you need right now is to miss that ferry!"

The two girls sat on the bench at the island's dock; as one of the last return trips of the day, it promised to be a crowded ride. Jade had insisted on purchasing a ticket and riding back to the Michigan mainland with Ellen, presumably in hopes of buffering Ellen from the offended owner of the Celtic Inn.

"This was one of the best days of my life," Ellen said in a hushed voice.

"Sure. Me too," said Jade as she leaned sideways to rest her cheek on top of Ellen's head. There was no doubt they had made a connection. "I believe you. You know that, right?" Ellen drew back, peering into her friend's face. Jade returned her look with all seriousness now. "You're not the only one that's had visits from an angel."

"No, not me," Jade replied, as if sensing Ellen's question. A faraway look came into her eyes. "My mother—yes, she believed in angels."

"But not God?" Ellen whispered with tears in her eyes.

"Honestly, I'm not sure," said Jade. And as she leaned her head down again, she surprised Ellen again by asking, "What about you? Do you believe in God?"

Ellen pulled away again, this time indignantly. "Of course I do! You've been hanging around horses so long you have manure in your ears!"

But Jade stayed the course, unoffended; her point demanded to be made. "I'm not convinced your actions match your words, young one," she said sagely.

Ellen chose to take a page from her companion's book, letting go of any anger at a chance of gleaning some wisdom. "I'm listening," she said with a husky voice.

Jade's next words poured like liquid truth into the cracks of her wounded heart. "If this God of yours loves you so much, why is that not enough? He has provided you with a loving family. Why must you keep searching? If he is all that you say, his greatest hope for you would be to find contentment. Stop looking beyond your own heart. Is he not there?"

He *was* in her heart, and all at once, Ellen was ready to experience his love and mercy like never before. The pieces were dropping swiftly into place; now she knew why God had sent Esterlynn. He had provided a way for her to meet this mysterious young woman, a most unlikely source to give her closure. Her search was over. It was time to go home. The only mom she ever needed was there, along with her dad and sister. It was time to live the life God had planned for her.

Twenty-two

It was hard to believe the summer was pushing its way into mid-August already. Ellen was surrounded by neatly sorted piles of back-to-school supplies, purchased weeks ahead, courtesy of her mother's meticulous nature. As Ellen absentmindedly sharpened her pack of pencils, she found herself ruminating over the events of the summer.

She recalled her return to the St. Ignace dock that evening in early July, with Muriel anxiously awaiting the ferry's arrival. Ellen, prepared for an all-out lecture, had been taken aback by the older woman's response: the plan to use Jade as a buffer boasted brilliance because Muriel seemed more interested in Jade than Ellen. As the Chinese girls said their good-byes, Ellen kept thinking she saw a look in Muriel's eyes, one she could not quite identify.

Time would not allow for more than a few parting words. "Anyway, good luck in school," Ellen said to Jade, suddenly shy.

Muriel cut in before Jade could have a chance to respond. "Oh, me dear, God and luck don't go together." She gave Ellen's shoulders a squeeze.

Jade gave the Scottish woman a quizzical look but made no comment. Without reserve, Muriel pulled Jade into a swift embrace and with a tear-choked voice said, "Thank you, dear one, for watching out for me Ellen here. This was no luck. This here was a divine appointment by God himself."

And then, as quickly as Jade had entered her life, she was gone again—blending in with the other passengers on the last ferry to Mackinac Island for the day. The duo on the dock waved to Jade as she stood on the upper deck. Freezing the moment in her mind, Ellen found herself wondering if she'd ever see this exceptional young woman (or dare she say *soul mate)* again.

The next morning, after Muriel had served her guests, she and Ellen lingered over toast and eggs while they waited for Terri and Gwen to arrive. Ellen was feeling quite emotional about the whole trip and was sad to say good-bye to her hostess who had become such a good friend and mentor. She told Muriel of her remarkable experience with Esterlynn that evening after the party and how she sensed God telling her to go to the island. "I think I was sent to meet Jade," she said tentatively. "Does that sound crazy?"

Silence stretched and Ellen noticed Muriel had her eyes closed. Had she dozed off or was she praying perhaps? Without opening her eyes, she replied, "No, not crazy, me dear. Not crazy at all."

The women pulled up around 10:00 a.m. Terri and Muriel hit it off immediately. Ellen wasn't sure her mom would ever stop thanking the B & B's owner, with Muriel insisting Ellen had been more of a help than a guest and she was welcome to come back anytime.

By mid-afternoon, Terri had taken the driver's seat on the way back to Wisconsin. Gwen suggested they have coffee at the truck stop in Manistique. Ellen was thrilled by this idea, hoping secretly that she might recover her bag and money. The waitress they'd had that day was not working and after checking the lost-and-found, no lost, monogrammed bags had been reported. Inquiring about Chuck only produced another mystery. Madge, unbeknownst as the only one with information on Chuck, had worked the early morning shift.

Jack had flown in from LA and made it home within an hour of Ellen's homecoming. The Sattler family, including Gwen of course, had pizzas delivered with ice cream for dessert. It was a joyous occasion with lots of laughter and the usual fun-poking that only works between the closest of families. Ellen's trip to Mackinac Island was never mentioned, nor her meeting with Jade. Bless her heart; Muriel must have decided to keep that little secret between them.

The rest of the summer had included family trips to Devil's Lake Campground and a weekend at Noah's Ark Waterpark. Ellen and Emily took swimming lessons together at the local pool and went horseback riding at her cousin's farm.

All in all, it was an amazing summer for young Ellen. But the greatest gift of all was the change that was happening in her heart. Having found a closer relationship with Jesus had brought clarity to her world that had been missing before. She was amazed by God's goodness and sensed his presence in a new way; she no longer felt alone or incomplete.

Yes, indeed, it had been a miraculous summer. She finished sharpening her last pencil, setting it at the end of the neat row on the table. She gazed out the patio doors at the hazy scene of summer in August, her ears picking up the low hum of the central air unit. As she often did, she found herself wondering about Chuck. She removed her angel pin and gazed at it for the hundredth time. As with Jade, Ellen hoped to meet up with him again someday. As it turned out, someday would be sooner than she thought.

Twenty-three

Chuck used his key to open the front door to The Coffee House, leaving the CLOSED sign turned toward the street; it would be another hour before they opened. He scanned the checklist affixed to the wall just inside the kitchen area, things that needed to be done before they opened at 8:00 a.m. More than two months had passed since he started working, but he still needed those cues to keep him on track. All these foo-foo coffee concoctions posed a challenge to his aging memory. In his day, a man drank his coffee black, or if he could pull off a Clint Eastwood-type persona, he might get away with adding a splash of cream. Now these young people ordered things like nonfat double lattes or Irish crème espressos for a mere five bucks a pop! But who was he to complain? The expensive habits of the local college crowd kept him in regular paychecks.

Chuck reluctantly hung his Harley Davidson hat on a hook in the back break area. He wore black pants and shoes with a sage-green polo. The shirt (also available in red, mustard yellow, or navy blue) bore The Coffee House logo. At sixty-two years old, Chuck determined the day he wore mustard yellow would be the day he risked living on the streets!

Shaking off his grumbling thoughts, Chuck took his Bible into the restaurant area and sat in his favorite spot, a high stool at the end of the counter; here is where he read the Word, praying and meditating on God's truth. He'd been asking God every day about Ellen and the money he owed her. Shortly after arriving in Sault Saint Marie, he'd gone back to the library, searching online for Sattlers in the Fox River Valley of Wisconsin. He'd found one Jack Sattler, married to Terri; at one time in his brief encounter with Gwen and Ellen, he was sure Gwen had mentioned her brother's name was Jack. He pulled the piece of paper out of his Bible and stared at it again; right there in his own neat print was Ellen Sattler's address. There was no earthly reason not to mail the money to Ellen, even if his budget necessitated small deposits for now, but Chuck wasn't following his own human understanding; he was following the voice of the Holy Spirit. And the Holy Spirit was telling him to wait. No matter how many different ways he asked why, he only heard that one word: *wait*.

He finished his time with God, asking as always for opportunities to love the people that came through the door—if possible, to share the good news of Christ to those who did not know him. He slid the stool back into position, in perfect line with the others at the counter. He glanced around the room before reviewing the checklist. He could understand why the kids liked to hang out here. It had a very cozy feel with tables and chairs at one end near shelves of board games. Next to a group of overstuffed chairs stood a piano that remembered days past when its keys produced music in tune. The other end of the narrow room had a bank of five computers providing free Internet access for paying customers. On the counter near the window was a collection of random books for reading in house; these included a variety of local history, new-age art, religious topics, and classic novels. Chuck had never seen a single one touched since he'd been there.

He finished prepping everything for the day, step-by-step according to the list used for opening the store. Unlocking the front door and turning the sign to OPEN, Chuck went outside to wipe a rag over the few outdoor tables with chairs. He was watering the pots of flowers when he saw his coworker heading toward him.

Regan was doing her own little dance step as she made her way to The Coffee House, her ear buds playing an inaudible tune. The young woman sang indiscriminately loud and off-key to a song no one else could recognize. Chuck noticed she was once again toting her roommate's computer bag. The coffee shop closed daily at 2:00 p.m. and on Saturdays Regan often took advantage of the afterhours quiet to study.

Chuck held the door for her with his right hand and raised his left in greeting. As if suddenly realizing where she was, Regan's lips (painted fire-engine red) parted into a grin, showing off her perfect, post-braced teeth. "Well, thank you, kind sir," she said with a flourish and a half-curtsy.

He watched her head to the back room to put away her purse and computer. Today she wore a black skirt, not quite covering her knees, with bare legs and sandaled feet. Not exactly Coffee House-approved apparel, but she was at least wearing the standard polo—bright red to match her lipstick.

"Hey, Chuck. Ready for another exciting day at everyone's favorite Starbucks knockoff?" she asked.

Chuck was used to the girl's sarcasm and chose to ignore it. Regan was a student at Lake Superior State University, hoping to become a nurse. The streaks of red in her otherwise blonde hair, along with the nose and eyebrow piercings, didn't exactly speak to any sort of bedside manner, but certainly more outlandish things were known to happen.

"I thank God for another day. And for you, Regan" were Chuck's customary words to this young, unsaved girl.

Regan headed for the sound system and cranked it up. "Sure, Chuck. Let's see if God wants to rock this joint."

The morning progressed with the usual coffee-farers, Saturday bringing a mix of college students and business-type customers. A variety of fresh pastries enticed the early morning crowd from the display case, brought in daily from the neighboring bakery. Chad punched in at eleven, working the kitchen for the lunch crowd; The Coffee House served a limited menu of soups, salads, and sandwiches.

Regan punched out at exactly 2:00 p.m. and hauled her computer to a table near an outlet. Chuck locked the door and flipped the OPEN sign back to CLOSED. Some days, he chatted with lingering customers, but today, the shop was barren but for him and Regan. He busied himself for a while, wiping down menus and restocking the condiment area. The manager would stop in soon to take care of the cash register.

He glanced at Regan as he headed to the back to retrieve his favored hat. Fixing her makeup from a small compact looked to be a higher priority than her studies. He walked past the future Florence Nightingale with her fresh coat of lipstick and was about to remind her to lock the door behind him when his eyes caught hold of the wallpaper on the computer screen. He moved in closer, not able to believe his eyes. His heart picked up pace even as his knees tried to buckle. Forgetting in his excitement that it was not Regan's computer, he found himself nearly shouting, "How do you know them?" His wide and unblinking eyes refused to be torn from the monitor.

Regan seemed somewhat startled by Chuck's intensity. He had an almost wild look as he stared at the screen. "That's my roommate," she said.

Chuck's mind did a slight tilt as he took in the details of the photo. The older girl, apparently Regan's roommate, stood casually with a beautiful and serene smile on her face. Even dressed in casual clothes, something about her declared a look of elegance. But as captivating as she was, the roommate was not the object of his attention; her arm was slung in a most carefree fashion around the shoulders of a young Chinese girl. As sure as he was born, Chuck found himself looking into the happy face of his young friend and benefactor, Ellen Sattler.

Regan told Chuck what she knew about the photo, which wasn't much. Jade had worked the summer as a carriage driver on Mackinac Island. Apparently, she'd met the young Chinese girl, touring the island alone, and had befriended her for the day. Regan didn't even know the kid's name. Chuck proceeded to tell Regan about his meeting with Ellen, including the fact that she bore his deceased wife's namesake. So excited was he at this discovery that he found himself telling his young coworker about the pin he'd given Ellen, the one belonging to his Ellen.

Regan leaned in toward the picture, eyes all squinty. "Whoa, that's spooky!" Her eyes widened as she tapped the screen with her perfectly manicured nail. Chuck pulled his cheaters from his pocket. A brilliant smile broke wide across his weathered face as he saw it—the tiniest hint of gold on Ellen's shirt—near her collarbone. She was wearing the pin!

Chuck patted Regan gently on the shoulder as he leaned back. "No, my dear, that is not in any sense of the word 'spooky.' *That* is what Christians call a divine connection." His head still whirling, he found himself laughing out loud at the very goodness of God. But even then he began to wonder if this was some sort of sign, a shift in direction perhaps? He was anxious to get alone with God and ask what this new development meant. Was he destined to meet the roommate? Perhaps talking with Jade would help to clarify why God had been telling him to wait.

Neither Chuck nor Regan had any way of knowing that the older Chinese girl in the picture would never meet Chuck. Neither knew that Jade's time on earth would in fact be complete before the next sunrise.

Twenty-four

Two weeks later, Chuck was sitting in his usual spot before-hours at The Coffee House. He closed his Bible and laid one rough hand on its worn cover. Large tears sporadically peppered his hand as he leaned into the counter, head hanging over the ancient Word. He was still struggling to hear God's voice through the rush of events since that day he saw the picture.

A fatality was hard not to notice in a town the size of Sault Saint Marie. The pastor at the church he'd been attending mentioned it first: a late-night accident, a college student crossing the street on her bike and being struck by a car that was exceeding the speed limit. No evidence to support whether the driver was intoxicated or not just yet, but the girl died in the ambulance on the way to the hospital, from a combination of massive head injuries and internal bleeding. Chuck's heart went out to the family of the young girl as the pastor led his flock in prayer. But it wasn't until he was walking back to his motel room after service that he saw the picture on the front page of the local paper at the stand outside the gas station.

Oh Lord, no! The words didn't come out audibly; it was more of a moan from his spirit. After the initial shock of seeing Jade's face as the victim of the previous night's accident, Chuck found himself praying immediately for both Ellen and Regan. Surely, Ellen didn't know yet, but what about Regan? The Coffee House was closed on Sundays, but something told him to go there anyway.

Sure enough, there was Regan, sitting at one of the outdoor tables, face buried in her hands. As he pulled a chair next to hers, it made a horrible scraping noise. This was followed by a loud moment of noiselessness, a piercing quiet that hung like a wet sheet on the line without the slightest breeze to lift its weight and break the silence. At some point, he allowed himself to wrap one arm around her shoulders and give a gentle squeeze. No words were needed, but this fatherly gesture opened the grieving floodgate. Regan sobbed openly as she laid her head on his shoulder, even as his arm held her tighter.

And in the land where the living move forward without the dead, arrangements were made. There would be no burial in Michigan; Jade's body would be flown home to her family in China. A memorial service was held at the college for students and faculty to honor and say good-bye to this young freshman that few people had had a chance to know. One of Jade's professors had asked Regan to say a few words, but she had declined, admitting only to Chuck that she really didn't know the deep but private girl who'd been her roommate for a short time.

Now, as Chuck cried and prayed over his Bible, he heard a tapping on the front window of the coffee shop; Regan peered at him through the glass, evidence that she'd once again forgotten her key. As he turned the deadbolt and opened the door, he was relieved to see that his young coworker looked better today. At first he chalked it up to two weeks' time since the accident, but then he realized it was more than that; there was a look in her eyes that actually bore what he could only perceive as excitement.

He raised his eyebrows in a questioning manner and had no time to speak before she pulled an envelope from her handbag, thrusting it urgently toward his hands. Again, he merely raised his eyebrows. "Okay," she started, "you know how I've been going through some of Jade's computer files before the university ships it to China with her other stuff?" There would be no waiting for his acknowledgement, as she was clearly unable to contain herself. "Well, let's just say I ran across a file that's gonna blow that treasured Harley hat right off your head!"

Her eyes were quite alive and dancing as she suddenly pulled the envelope out of his reach and returned it to the depths of her bag. "You know what, Chuck? You'll be useless to the customers today if you read this first. I think it's best you take it with you and read it at home after closing." Regan nodded to herself, obviously pleased with her decision, as if she were his mother or something.

Chuck knew enough about women to realize it would be easier to wait than to argue. But later that day, even as he closed and locked the door of his hotel room, he found his hands shaking as he stared at the envelope, suddenly not so sure he was ready to expose himself to its secrets. He closed his eyes and prayed. "Lord, you've trusted me with this information for some reason. Make it clear to me how you would have me respond to whatever it is that I am about to discover."

Ever so slowly, Chuck opened the envelope and pulled out the folded sheets of paper with a strange mixture of fear and excitement. He was typically a fast reader anyway, and after scanning the first few sentences, he found himself wanting to hurry to the end. But as he realized the implications of this letter, he forced himself to close his eyes again, praying for several minutes before continuing.

He read the letter three times thoroughly before setting it gently on the bed. He walked over to the dingy window without noticing its dinginess. Two words of affirmation were spoken. "Okay then." Saying it aloud might give him the conviction to do the very thing that was demanding to be done.

It was time to go to Wisconsin; his reunion with Ellen Sattler was nigh.

Twenty-five

It was a beautiful Saturday morning in early October and the leaves were just starting to hit their peak in brilliant color saturation in northeastern Wisconsin. Chuck was singing hymns of worship as he walked, hoping to keep at bay the anxious thoughts threatening to gnaw at his mind. How does one deliver such news? His prayers had consisted of giving it up to God, over and over. "Lord, I will trust in you with all my heart. I will not lean on my own understanding. In all my ways, I will acknowledge you and you will direct my paths."

He'd requested time off at work and hitched several rides from Sault Saint Marie to the Green Bay area. Thursday afternoon was his last ride—a Schneider truck driver had dropped him at a gas station on the west side of town. He found Green Bay to be an expanding area with heavy focus on industry, including several large paper mills along the Fox River. The people seemed friendly enough, and a kind, young woman loaned him her cell phone to make the call.

Terri Sattler had answered the phone and managed to maintain a level of professionalism, even as her voice was laced with uneasiness. Their brief discussion revealed that Ellen had indeed heard about Jade's death; apparently, the owners of the B & B in St. Ignace heard the report and relayed the news to Gwen. This much was a relief on Chuck's part—the worst blow already delivered. He asked Terri if he might stop by to meet both her and Jack and share more information about Jade, explaining his connection through Regan. Somewhat reluctantly, Terri conceded and told Chuck that Jack wouldn't be home until Friday night but he was welcome to come Saturday morning.

Having two nights to wait, he checked into an affordable hotel. Friday was a day of waiting, and if he'd had the funds, he might have toured the famous Lambeau Field or other local attractions. Instead, he strolled through the neighborhood near his hotel, sitting for hours at a local park, enjoying the young toddlers playing with their moms. He thought of his Ellen a lot that day, wondering how she would handle this whole thing. He had no doubt her words would be seasoned with salt and filled with love and grace. Oh, how he wished she were here with him!

Now, at long last, it was Saturday morning. Before leaving Michigan, he'd printed detailed maps at the library and researched the current construction areas. It seemed appropriate to finish his journey on foot, taking the back roads for nearly ten miles to the more rural area where the Sattlers lived. Finally, after nearly four hours of walking, he came upon their home. Settled back a good distance from the road was a ranch-style house with a three-car garage, looking to be around twenty years old. Gorgeous oak and maple trees shaded the front yard on a large lot that could easily cover three acres. He was so busy taking in the property as he walked up the long driveway that he didn't even notice Ellen sitting on a swing that hung from one of the larger oaks near the house.

She jumped from the swing, running with the swiftness of a gazelle. She nearly knocked him over as she tackled him with the type of hug shared between two very old and dear friends. His emotions bubbled over as he drew back to get a better look at his Chinese friend. Had it already been more than three months since they'd met? When he noticed her wearing the pin, he set down his pack and pulled out her monogrammed bag. The look of surprise on Ellen's face made Chuck laugh aloud. He explained his finding it at the diner and the struggle he'd faced to use her money as a loan. "The way I see it," he said, "God was using you to provide for this old scruff. No suspenders, remember?"

The radiant smile that broke across her face was soon confused by a curious sadness in her eyes. The weight of the uncertain purpose of his visit was reflected there. He hugged her again. "Everything's gonna be okay," he said. The empty platitude may have sounded absurd, but somehow he believed God would bring something good from all this. His Ellen used to say there was always joy, even in the painful things. Sometimes, it just took a little while to find it.

By now, mid-afternoon, the sun had warmed the backyard nicely; Jack and Terri had prepared a light lunch which they ate outside on the back patio. Brynn was there as well and the conversation was surprisingly easy even with the mystery of today's visit waiting in the wings. Jack and Chuck lingered over coffee (real coffee—not the yuppie stuff they served at The Coffee House) while the women cleared the table. Jack seemed especially interested in Chuck's work history and asked if he might be interested in finding a job in the Green Bay area, having more opportunities in a bigger city. "Also," he said with a grin, "I have a feeling my daughter and my sister would love to have you living closer."

The afternoon was wearing on as chitchat was served back and forth in ping-pong fashion, with Ellen and Chuck reliving the day they met on the highway and Ellen filling Chuck in on her adventures in the St. Ignace area. There was no telling how long this would have gone on if not for the look that Terri kept throwing Jack's way. The look that said, "Can we get on with this?"

It was cooling off by now, and Jack suggested they move to the living room. "This has been a wonderful afternoon, getting to know you, Chuck. We want to thank you for coming all this way for whatever it is you have to share with us."

Chuck admired Jack's candor and was as ready as he would ever be to oblige everyone with the purpose of his mission. He pulled a photo from his pack and handed it to Ellen. It was the one from Jade's wallpaper, printed by Regan. Ellen's eyes filled with tears even as she smiled in memory. "Jerome took this picture," she said.

"Who's Jerome, honey?" Terri asked as she moved next to her daughter to get a closer look.

"He's one of the guys that worked in the stable with Jade." Tears poured down her cheeks. "I forgot he took this."

Chuck gave them a minute before he went on with his story. He told them about seeing the picture on the computer just the day before Jade died. He looked down at his hands for a moment before explaining about the files Regan had sorted through on Jade's computer. At this point, he pulled the sheets of paper from his pack. "After readin' this, I figured it was best for me to bring it in person. It's from some sort of journal she kept, dated July fifth of this year." Looking to Ellen, he asked, "That's the day you met Jade, right?" Ellen only nodded. "You want me to read it to you, or maybe your mom or dad?"

"What do you think, Cookie?" asked Jack.

The young girl managed to remain brave. "Go ahead, Chuck."

He cleared his throat and set his cheaters on the tip of his nose. He was deathly silent in that eternal second before he began.

> Today started like any other day. Woke early, showered, and ate my usual breakfast of grapefruit

and dry toast before taking my bike to the stables. I did my usual morning tours, met some more interesting people. The newlyweds from Montana were especially sweet and amusing. It's my job to entertain these groups, but once in a while, a couple like that comes along and steals the show. I don't mind really. Makes my job easier by enhancing my "performance." Ha! Maybe I should become an actor!

Anyway, it was late morning and I was heading out on the final tour of my shift. As often happens, I stopped in front of The Grand to give Gunther and Lady a break before pulling up the hill. That's when I saw her. She was sitting in the shade near the road, looking right at me. It was like looking into a mirror. We stared at each other until Gunther started bobbing his head in that fashion that tells me he's ready to go. I forced my mind back to my job as we headed up the hill, but I couldn't shake the feeling that I'd seen a ghost.

Later, after Gunther and Lady were settled in the stable, I decided to bike downtown. I'm still not sure why. It's not my usual habit, but I felt compelled. I suppose Ellen would say God led me there.

So there she was again, sitting down near the water, eating fudge and watching the parade of kites. I'm not sure how long I stood there, watching her from a distance, afraid of what I thought I might find but more afraid that I wouldn't. Realizing I would never have this chance again, and knowing I needed to know, I walked up and said hello. My mouth went dry when she turned toward me. The whole idea had been crazy, yet the evidence said differently when I saw the telltale birthmark hugging the right side of her face and neck. How could it be?

We spent the day together—a wonderful, magical day. My conscience seemed to say I should tell her, but I couldn't. Even now—as I write this from my room on the island and she is somewhere across the lake at a B & B—I don't know why I didn't. Maybe it was the way she came off as so completely vulnerable. Maybe I was afraid she wouldn't believe me. But really, I think it was about not wanting to ruin the new level of acceptance she seemed to have found for her adopted family today. Maybe that really was why we met. Maybe she really did have an angel guiding her. That story alone opened a huge window for me to tell her the truth. The angel that visited my mother, as she claimed, showed up on an annual basis: every year on the anniversary of the day she gave up her daughter—her second daughter.

It was a terrible day, one of hope and fear and loss all tangled together. My mother's labor had begun in the middle of the night, and my aunt stayed to comfort her and monitor her progress. It wasn't until the child was ready to be born that other women from the village showed up to assist. The baby was born healthy. The bright eyes and fine hair could not distract from the birthmark, or more importantly, the fact that the child was indeed a girl.

I was ten years old when my little sister was born. It was a heartbreaking thing for me—watching my mother nurse her baby and stroke her cheek, knowing what would come next. I really believe she was in denial at first, not willing to accept or even remember the fact that she could not keep this child. It took several days before the reality of what she must do started to sink in. In that region, at that time, families were only allowed two children. If she had any hope of having a boy to help with the planting and one day help to financially support the family, she would have to give up her new baby girl.

Strangers took my baby sister to the city. Our family never knew what became of her. We only had our hope, as other families like ours did, that somehow she would be cared for, maybe even adopted. My baby brother was born a few years later. My parents loved him, but my mother never lost that vacant look that came into her eyes the day she said good-bye to her daughter. No one could comfort her loss but the visits from her angel kept her going. Did the angel somehow assure her that her child was okay? She would never say.

And so, all these years later, my mother gone now, I find myself reunited with her daughter, halfway across the world. My day started in a most expected way, with grapefruit and toast, but it ended with my sister and me (Wow! Yes! My sister and me!) riding the ferry together! How could my life ever be the same? Maybe someday I will see her again and I can tell her that I didn't lie when I told Jerome that she was my sister. Somehow, that seems important, that my sister would know that I didn't lie. Also, strange

> *as it may sound—only spending one day together—I fell in love with her.*

As Chuck finished reading, there was a sense of the final curtain of a play being reopened. No cast members would appear for a last applause this time. The stage was empty yet crying out for another scene.

Twenty-six

Autumn rains moved in later that day, adding to the gloominess that hung over the Sattler home. After a great deal of resistance, Chuck had finally consented to his personal delivery back to Michigan. The Sattlers insisted it was the least they could do after Chuck hitched his way all the way down here to deliver the letter. Jack needed to be back for an early flight to LA Monday morning but Gwen had agreed to ride with her brother to share the driving. It was about a nine-hour drive one way to Sault Saint Marie; Gwen and Jack would take turns driving through the night and more or less straight back the next day.

They'd been gone for a while now and Ellen was tucked into her bed. Even her favorite flannel PJs could not quell the shiver seeping into her bones, its source not the damp weather. The sensation was more from the inside out. Sleep came and went; the voices of her mother and Brynn whispered off and on, apparently keeping vigil. Mere hours had passed, but in her confused state, time seemed to tilt sideways. She must have been having a nightmare because her mom came in and sat on the edge of her bed, gently brushing her hair from her forehead. "I'm right here, baby. Mommy's here."

"I'm so cold, Mommy," she whispered.

Terri drew back the covers. Ellen moved to the edge of the narrow twin bed so her mom could crawl in beside her; this slight regression seemed permissible, this fragile girl of ten receiving such an emotional blow. Terri wrapped her arms around her daughter as she began to sing. It was the song she had sung to Ellen from the earliest days, even cradling her as a baby on that flight from China to the United States. "Raindrops on roses and whiskers on kittens—" she sang softly. To this day Terri could not recall how she had chosen that song from *The Sound of Music*, yet it always did the trick. Even now, she could feel Ellen relax, if only slightly, in her embrace.

Terri prayed as she sang, waiting for Ellen to talk first if words were indeed needed in that moment. She stopped singing but continued to hum the tune, hugging her child with the breaking heart. Three soft words poured forth at last. "Just one day."

"I know, honey, but some day, you will see that God gave you a gift. Even that one day you would not have, if not for Esterlynn." Terri felt warm tears running down her cheeks and spilling into Ellen's hair, helpless to take her daughter's pain as her own.

"It doesn't feel like a *gift!*" she cried angrily. "God didn't give me anything. He took her from me! Why would he do that, Mom?"

"I don't know, Ellen. Some things God does not allow us to see; these are the challenges that allow us to trust him more, if we choose to. Every struggle we go through in life is an opportunity to grow our character and to learn more about the nature of who God really is."

"I don't like God very much right now, Mom." These were her last words before she broke into angry sobs of grief.

Terri held her tighter and rocked her gently; the time for words had expired. As a mother, her heart was aching, but that same experienced heart was hearing the voice of the Holy Spirit quite clearly. *Hope will come from this.* She wouldn't bother sharing this with Ellen; she wouldn't have believed it anyway. But Terri believed, and she would be watching.

It was just before dawn in Sault Saint Marie and the sun seemed to toy with the idea of starting another day, as if it had a choice. Chuck didn't bother inviting his friends in; they were eager to retrace their miles, and there was really nothing left to say.

"Good to see you again, Gwen. I miss the pink hat," he said with a sad laugh.

"You're a good man, Chuck. If I didn't know you better, I'd ask to borrow your Harley hat." She returned his serve with her own volley of futile humor. They hugged without awkwardness for a long moment.

"Thanks for everything, Chuck. And she'll be okay, you know," Jack said from behind them. Even as he said it, he recognized how strange it was that he—Ellen's father—would be reassuring this stranger. Yet he didn't feel like a stranger, even from that first handshake the day before; Jack had a strong sense this experience would add Chuck to the ranks of the Sattler family. Only God could have ordained this union that began with his sister picking up a "bum" on the side of the road during a summer storm!

Chuck waved until their car reached the end of the street and turned from his sight. Bone weary, he climbed the stairs to his motel room. Not bothering to pull back the covers, he eased himself down and stretched his body the entire length of the bed. His suspicion that sleep would evade him proved wrong. He'd barely started praying for the Sattler family—for the trying times ahead and for the healing that only God could provide—before he dropped off into a deep sleep laced with a combination of sadness and satisfaction.

Twenty-seven

It was Thanksgiving Day. About seven weeks had passed since Chuck's visit and his *dropping the bomb,* as Ellen liked to think of it. Her mom's sister and husband had driven up from the Milwaukee area, bringing her grandma in tow as was tradition for the holiday. Thanksgiving had always been one of Ellen's favorite days, a somewhat peaceful and serene springboard into the more hectic season of Christmas and New Year's.

But this year was different. Confusion and a sense of unrest were heavy upon the young girl. Ellen had been seeing a counselor once a week. Kathy had been recommended by the school counselor, and while she seemed a very nice lady, Ellen couldn't seem to communicate what it was that remained unresolved in her heart. With no apparent results on the horizon, the only thing she seemed to be gaining was a rise in her frustration level.

The result of putting all that in a bag and shaking it with the missed ideal of Thanksgiving pushed Ellen to take a walk. An early snow had arrived over the weekend—at least four inches. She pulled on her boots and heavy coat. Wrapping a warm woolen scarf around her head and neck, she let herself out the back door. She had no particular mind as to where she was going.

But as God often has it, when one of his children is cloudy in thought (or one might say lost), he calls upon someone close to that person, someone who would know their thoughts, to bring them back.

Not too many people had visited the cemetery since the snowfall, which made it conveniently easy for Brynn to find Ellen's tracks. Somehow, she knew this was where her sister would be, although she wasn't sure exactly where Esterlynn had made her debut. The remainder of light from the cloudy day was fading toward dusk already as she followed Ellen's tracks into the graveyard. Brynn had sent Gwen a text as soon as she'd confirmed her suspicion on Ellen's location, her aunt promising to be here soon.

The small boot prints made a sharp turn to the left. Brynn paused to take in the scene. Faint in the distance was Ellen, head bowed with knees in the snow—at the feet of Christ crucified. Brynn approached slowly, quietly, expecting to hear soft sobs or an outright heaving of her young sister's soul. But as she closed the gap, she saw Ellen shift her gaze toward the face of Jesus and tip her head slightly, as if listening. Brynn halted now, not wanting to interrupt this exchange, whatever it might be. Ellen seemed to sense her presence, however, and turned to face her sister.

Without a word, Brynn covered the last few yards separating them and simply kneeled next to Ellen in the cold snow. They stayed that way, not a word passing between them for several long minutes, before Ellen surprised Brynn with her first sentiment. "You will always be my sister, Brynn."

And so it was that the older sister found herself to be the one dropping hot tears into the snow. "Thanks, kiddo. I think I needed to hear that." Silence begged center stage a little longer before

Brynn finally said, "It looked like you were listening to someone. Was it Esterlynn?"

A shadow of uncertainty crossed Ellen's face. "I'm not sure. I didn't see Esterlynn like the other times, but I thought I heard a voice."

"What did it say?" Brynn asked.

"I'm not sure I understand it," said Ellen. "But what I heard was 'Why do you seek the living among the dead?'"

At that moment, both girls jumped as a voice from behind them plainly said, "That wasn't Esterlynn." The sisters scrambled to their feet and turned to see Gwen, her rose-colored Sorrels attempting to match but only clashing with her pink earmuffs and mittens.

"Gwen!" Ellen cried with surprise and relief. "If it wasn't Esterlynn, who was it?"

Gwen took two steps forward and patted Ellen's cheek with her mittened hand. "My dear, God is showing you that you don't need Esterlynn anymore. That was the Holy Spirit speaking Scripture to your heart. It's from the gospel of Luke."

Ellen opened her mouth to respond but Gwen shifted her mitten, gently patting the young girl's lips. "It's time for us to have a talk. I'll explain everything but not in this frozen wasteland. Come along, girls. We'll have some hot chocolate at my house."

Twenty-eight

Being late November, the days were shortening, and it was nearly dark already as they gathered in the cozy family room. Gwen's house felt more like a cottage than a house. Her furniture was circa 1975 with its bright, flowered patterns and an overstuffed look, which cleverly disguised the fact that it was truly uncomfortable. They sat in front of the fireplace where Gwen had built a *real* fire, as she put it; gas fireplaces were making wood-burning ones a dying breed, forcing the very skill of fire building to near extinction.

There was some light banter at first as the bag of marshmallows was passed back and forth, mugs piled high to overflowing. The girls settled a bit as Gwen told the resurrection story from Luke about the two angels at the tomb, asking the women why they sought the living among the dead. Imagine their joy at the next words that were spoken. "He is not here; he has risen!"

Ellen sipped her hot chocolate, gazing into the mesmerizing flames. Gwen gave her time, allowing her to process this and see if she would make the connection to what God was trying to tell her. "That cross at the cemetery—" she finally said. "Jesus isn't dead on the cross; he's alive in heaven with God, right?"

"That's true, Ellen, but I think the Holy Spirit gave you that Scripture for a much more personal reason. He wants to give you closure as far as Jade is concerned."

Ellen started crying harder than she had cried since Chuck had delivered the letter. At a loss, Brynn tried putting her arm around her sister, only to be pushed away. Her alarm grew as Ellen's voice escalated to a near scream. "Jade isn't alive. She's dead! She's not with Jesus; *she's just dead!*"

With some effort, Gwen moved from her chair and eased herself to the floor in front of Ellen; Brynn held her breath. Gwen looked willing to wait until the new year, if necessary, as the young girl poured out her deepest pain and regret. When she was able to speak, Ellen told them about her conversation that day with Jade on the island, the fact that Jade had not accepted Jesus as her Savior. "So now, she's gone and I can't bear to think of where she is!" The sobbing resumed.

Gwen leaned back a bit with a sad but satisfied smile on her face. "When you're ready, dear, I'll tell you the rest of the story, the good news."

Ellen raised her tear-filled gaze to lock with Gwen's. "There's *good* news?"

Gwen let out a classic chuckle that seemed to meld with the heat from the fire and dance around the room. "The day that you met Jade was also the day Jade met Muriel. Although you left town the next day, Jade and Muriel were destined to stay connected." Gwen allowed a delightful pause to hover as she watched the surprised looks on the sisters' faces.

Ellen's look went from surprise to confusion. "But how—?" she began.

"Muriel told me she had a sense about Jade. She said God would wake her up in the middle of the night with your biological sister pressing on her heart. This went on for several nights before Muriel decided to call Jade; she had her number on her caller ID from when you borrowed her phone, remember?"

Realization lit up Ellen's face, her eyes growing bright even as the tears were still drying on her face. "Yes, I remember! So they got together again!" She said it more as a statement than a question.

"Oh, they got together many times, Ellen. Muriel was careful not to push the girl. She simply met her for lunch a couple of times first; her primary goal was to gain her trust. And it worked."

Savoring the moment, Gwen looked back and forth between the faces of her anxious audience. "I think we need some snacks," she said with a slight grunt as she coaxed her resistant body off the floor.

Late afternoon passed into early evening. Jack and Terri were summoned and Gwen prepped a cheese and sausage tray while waiting their arrival. The Sattlers came with pumpkin pie and open ears, no one wanting to miss the story that had waited so long to be told.

Muriel would always say that prayer was the biggest factor during those weeks. She knew her time was short with Jade heading to Sault Saint Marie by mid-August. She started to make a breakthrough with Jade as she simply shared her own testimony, talking about how God had changed her life and given her strength through her trials. She often quoted Scripture, which really piqued Jade's interest, and when Muriel sensed the time was right, she gave Jade a Bible and helped her to understand the basics of its layout and suggested she start by reading the book of John. The day before Jade left for college, they met for breakfast—at McDonald's of all places! The Holy Spirit had done his work and Jade asked Muriel to explain how she could become a Christian. Right there, with the ruckus of toddlers in the adjacent play land, Jade prayed the sinner's prayer and accepted Christ as her Savior.

Gwen finished her story and smiled broadly at Ellen. "So you see, my dear, God used you to bring Muriel and Jade together. Sometimes, when we're right in the middle of things, it's hard to see what God is doing. This whole business with Esterlynn wasn't so much about you as it was about Jade. She is surely with Jesus now, and you were party to that. You were obedient to God's leading, and he is so proud of you."

Gwen looked at the faces around the room, faces reflecting love and amazement, before adding, "We're *all* proud of you."

Twenty-nine

It was Christmas Eve day. The hubbub of the holidays had kept everyone sufficiently preoccupied. Ellen had moved through the days since Thanksgiving with a strange mixture of joy and pain. The initial celebration of Jade's conversion was often overshadowed by the reality of simple human grief; the process would demand its course.

Today was one of her lighter days, knowing that Chuck would be arriving with Muriel and Ivan in time for the service at church that evening. The entire Sattler family had been thrilled when Jack's company offered Chuck a job. He'd be working in the machine shop department thirty hours a week with full benefits. Terri had done the legwork on apartment shopping in the area. Chuck would check out various complexes online and Terri would follow up with the apartment managers, touring prospective rentals and sending pictures via e-mail to Chuck.

It took less than two weeks for them to find a cozy two-bedroom on the second floor with a view of the Fox River. If all went as planned, the Sattlers would have him settled and employed by the new year. Muriel had agreed heartily to bring Chuck and his scant belongings down.

And so it was that the great reunion took place on this sacred night, the holiest one of the year: Christmas Eve. Gwen, Muriel, Ivan, and Chuck accompanied the Sattler family to their home church that evening. Ellen gazed at the angels on the stained glass above the altar with the same revelation of awe that she'd had since Thanksgiving. Although it was hard to make out the scene in the dark, her mind's eye could see it clearly. She'd spent countless Sundays since last spring memorizing every detail of their flowing blue gowns and cascading hair. The angels faced one another, mirror images, each blowing a horn so completely perfect tonight as they announced the birth of the Savior.

Pastor Steve gave the message, sandwiched between traditional Christmas hymns and the angelic anthem of the choir. A deep sense of contentment washed over Ellen as her ears absorbed the pastor's words from Matthew 5:8. "Blessed are the pure in heart, for they shall see God." Her heart had been tainted with resentment that day she'd met Esterlynn in the cemetery, but God, in his grace, had taken her on a journey of truth. Through his healing power, she had indeed adopted an attitude of gratitude that had softened her heart and made it pure. The result was glorious. Ellen now saw the goodness of God.

After church, everyone headed back to the Sattler home for hot cider and copious platters of Christmas treats. Gwen had brought her famous five-alarm chili. Laughter filled the air, the perfect accompaniment to the beautiful Christmas music floating from Terri's new Bose sound system in the background (an early Christmas gift from Jack).The enamored husband swept in, dancing his wife to a convenient halt underneath the mistletoe, everyone cheering as Terri's face flushed to a light scarlet color.

The tree was proudly adorned with a new angel, a gift to the family from Chuck; no doubt it would forever be a reminder of that Christmas of new beginnings. This was where Muriel found Ellen brushing a few stray tears with the back of her hand. She gave Ellen a brief hug before holding out a white envelope. "Open it, me dear."

Ellen cast a quizzical look at the Scottish matron before complying. Her hands shook slightly as she pulled a card from its unmarked casing. It was one of those bulky cards, which meant it had some sort of audio device embedded within. The front revealed a beautiful angel in a sparkling robe, head circled with a radiant glow of light. Her breathing slowed to nearly nothing as she opened the card.

Jade's beautiful voice said, "God is good!"

Muriel replied, "All the time!"

Jade echoed, "All the time!"

Muriel responded, "God is good!"

This declaration was punctuated with a chorus of laughter. In closure, they announced in joyous unison, "Merry Christmas, Ellen! We love you!"

Muriel explained that she and Jade had ordered the card online just before Jade left for college. Seeing the look on Ellen's face, Muriel said, "My sweet child, it was all in fun. But God knew."

Any semblance of holding her emotions together would have grandly failed at that point. Tears came with every thought and feeling she'd held in the past seven months. Leave it to God in his infinite knowledge of what was and is and is to come, to have provided her with this gift, a resurrected snippet of her sister's voice. A recording, though silly and insignificant at the time, now preserved a priceless treasure.

They hugged right there, in the shadow of the tree, with Chuck's angel smiling down on them. "Oh Muriel, God *is* good!"

"All the time, Ellen. All the time."

Epilogue

Years later, Ellen learned that Jade's given name had been Lin, which literally translated to "beautiful jade." Now, ironically, she stood in the lobby of the White Swan Hotel, admiring the detail of the giant, three-mast ship chiseled from beautiful jade. This gorgeous sculpture, at least twenty feet long and standing close to seven feet tall, was the meeting place for the departing group photo of each adoptive family.

So absorbed in her memories, Ellen didn't notice the attractive young Chinese man drifting quietly behind her. "It always offers something new, doesn't it?" he said in reference to the ship.

Ellen turned and punched him playfully in the shoulder. "Honestly, Cheng! You always manage to sneak up on me!" But she was laughing as he pulled her into a polite embrace. "I'm so excited to see you! My families will be here in a bit for our final good-byes, and then you and I will have a chance to catch up."

As if speaking it into existence, families appeared from the elevators; carts were piled high with mounds of luggage, diaper bags, strollers, and shopping bags. At this point, parents had the look that Ellen had come to know very well. It spoke of joy and weariness, uncertainties and farewells, all mixed together and displayed in various forms, based on the personalities of each family. Cameras and cell phones were working overtime to capture last-minute memories. Ellen moved in to organize the group for the famous photo with the majestic jade ship as a backdrop.

As she handed back her armload of cameras to their respective owners, Ellen felt a gentle squeeze on her upper arm. She turned to see Janice with a mischievous grin on her face. "So are you going to introduce us to your good-looking mystery man?"

"Having such a childlike curiosity of your own will surely make you a wonderful mother, Janice," Ellen said with a laugh. She would miss this bold woman and her soft-spoken husband. Then, turning to the object of the woman's nosiness (for that's what it really was), Ellen said, "This is Cheng."

"It's so nice to meet you, Cheng," Janice said with exaggerated cordiality. "Karl and I are so pleased that you are courting such a treasure as our Ellen. Aren't we, Karl?"

A blush crossed the faces of Karl and Ellen in perfect unison.

Cheng moved in swiftly to dissolve the awkward assumption. "I have no doubt that some fortunate man will one day be subject to Ellen's affection, but I am not he. I'm her brother."

A comical look of pure shock skated over Janice's face, swiftly replaced by one of accusation as she looked at Ellen. "You never told me your parents adopted a boy too!"

This time both Cheng and Ellen laughed. "They didn't," she said. "Cheng is my *biological* brother." They both laughed some more as they watched the wheels in poor Janice's mind trying to come into alignment.

"But—how?" was all she could manage to say.

"It's a long and wonderful story," Ellen said as Cheng wrapped his arm around her shoulders. "Someday, God willing, I can share it with you. Sadly, time is short and I must get these families outside to catch the shuttle." She gave Janice a warm hug before adding, "Let's just say, God is good."

Cheng closed with the proper response. "All the time."

All eleven families were on the curb now, waiting somewhat restlessly as the luggage was being loaded onto the shuttle that would take them to the airport. Some would fly to Beijing before heading north, over the globe to Chicago; others would have a layover in Tokyo before heading west.

An excited troop of "grandmas" filtered into the departing group. These were local Chinese women that spoke little if any English; their self-designated job was to check and make sure these American-bound babies were dressed with the proper layering of clothes. They also loved to fawn over the babies, sometimes simply touching them or more often asking to hold them. A big fuss was made as they smiled and spoke the same two words used to dub every adopted child, "lucky baby."

Karl politely waited until they were out of earshot before making one of his rare but profound statements. "Luck is for horseshoes and leprechauns."

Ellen looked at the man holding his newly adopted baby girl; the bonding process was moving along nicely. She held out her slender hands, palms turned skyward to cradle this precious child one last time. "May I?" she asked.

One of her all-time-favorite Bible verses came to mind as she cradled Sarah in the crook of her arm. Cheng hovered ever so near as Ellen leaned in, her face mere inches from the baby's. Her long, black hair fell like a silk curtain around Sarah's face, as if joining their similar fate, if only for a moment.

Inspired by Karl's words and her own spiritual prompting, Ellen breathed out the words from the book of James. "Every good and perfect gift is from above, coming down from the Father of the heavenly lights, who does not change like shifting shadows." And shaking her hair back, she added, "It has nothing to do with luck."

The baby reached up and patted Ellen's lips; their gaze held, unblinking. Then Sarah replied with a soft gurgling sound, as if that were all the amen that need be spoken.

CPSIA information can be obtained
at www.ICGtesting.com
Printed in the USA
JSHW020912010322
23446JS00002B/9